THE FORTUNES

*Follow the lives and loves of a complex family
with a rich history and deep ties
in the Lone Star State*

FORTUNE'S HIDDEN TREASURES

A new branch of the Fortune family heads to idyllic
Emerald Ridge to solve a decades-long mystery
that died with their parents, and a mysterious loss
that upends their lives. Little do they know that
their hearts will never be the same!

FORTUNE'S FAKE MARRIAGE PLAN

Nothing's going to part widowed single dad
Jax Wellington from his beloved infant son. And
if it takes a marriage of convenience to the
daughter of the town's best-connected family? So
be it! But what's not convenient is how his beguiling
new bride soon tempts his long-shuttered heart...

Dear Reader,

Welcome to Emerald Ridge, Texas! Jax and Priscilla have recently both just arrived back in this affluent town, and while they never hung out together as teens, despite running in the same circles, they team up to fight for a good cause—to ensure Jax will be able to keep custody of his infant son.

This story speaks to me because it's about two people who seemingly have everything but are, as successful adults, just finding their purpose. And, once found, they give everything to fulfill that purpose. I was lucky to discover my calling at fourteen when I picked up a promotional copy of a Harlequin Romance novel at the checkout of my local grocery store. And then bought another and another. I'd found my hope on those pages. And through it, my purpose. I was going to write for Harlequin and spend my life putting out into the world what those books gave to me.

I got a lot of pats on the head over the next years, but I knew who I was and what I was going to do. Through the hardships, the rejections, the jobs I did to support myself while I kept writing, I never lost sight of my purpose. And here I am, thirty years into my life with Harlequin and still doing what I'm meant to do. While these books are larger than life, their message is true every single time. Love is real. It's the source of the greatest happiness. And it has the power to combat every obstacle in its path.

Happy reading!

Tara

FORTUNE'S FAKE MARRIAGE PLAN

TARA TAYLOR QUINN

THE FORTUNES OF TEXAS

Special thanks and acknowledgment
are given to Tara Taylor Quinn for her contribution to
The Fortunes of Texas: Fortune's Hidden Treasures miniseries.

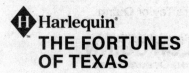

Harlequin®
THE FORTUNES OF TEXAS

Recycling programs
for this product may
not exist in your area.

ISBN-13: 978-1-335-14326-6

Fortune's Fake Marriage Plan

Copyright © 2025 by Harlequin Enterprises ULC

Harlequin Enterprises ULC
22 Adelaide St. West, 41st Floor
Toronto, Ontario M5H 4E3, Canada
www.Harlequin.com

Printed in Lithuania

MIX
Paper | Supporting
responsible forestry
FSC® C021394

A *USA TODAY* bestselling author of over one hundred novels in twenty languages, **Tara Taylor Quinn** has sold more than seven million copies. Known for her intense emotional fiction, Ms. Quinn's novels have received critical acclaim in the UK and most recently from Harvard. She is the recipient of the Readers' Choice Award and has appeared often on local and national TV, including *CBS Sunday Morning*. For TTQ offers, news and contests, visit tarataylorquinn.com!

Books by Tara Taylor Quinn

Harlequin Special Edition

The Cottages on Ocean Breeze

Beach Cottage Kisses

The Fortunes of Texas: Digging for Secrets

Fortune in Name Only

The Fortunes of Texas: Fortune's Hidden Treasures

Fortune's Fake Marriage Plan

Montana Mavericks: The Tenacity Social Club

Maverick's Full House

Visit the Author Profile page
at Harlequin.com for more titles.

For Sydney McDaniel, a transplanted Texan
who puts love first every single day.

Chapter One

A duck pond. That's what he needed on his land. Minus the ducks.

Natural waste every fifteen minutes, not good.

With a future curious toddler in the mix…no.

But the pond…with a greenway…helping to preserve the water's natural health…

"Jax."

At the not quite stern sound of his name, wealthy rancher Jax Wellington stood up from the ornate bench upon which he'd been sitting, staring at the park's duck pond.

So he didn't have to watch for the ex-in-laws who'd called the upcoming meeting.

Turning the stroller in which his three-month-old son slept so that its interior was facing him, he waited for Christa's parents, Emma and Frank Novelty, to reach him. And then, as if in pre-rehearsed synchronization, all three of them sat. Emma between Jax and her husband.

The immaculately dressed woman reached for the stroller and turned it so that it rested between her and Jax. Out of respect for the fact that they were grieving, and though his jaw was clenching, Jax recognized the childishness of his desire to assert that he was not only the boy's biological father, he was also Liam's only guardian, and thereby, the chooser of his son's whereabouts. In light of the Novelty's desire to share custody of his baby son, his defensiveness was understandable. Deliberate contention was not.

And he noted, with some appreciation, that Emma didn't reach down to pick up her sleeping grandson. Jax would have had to intervene to avoid a bout of some untimely and very loud expressions of dissatisfaction. His son had mastered the art of getting immediate attention when he was displeased.

As Jax had learned over and over again, every two hours, each night of the past month.

The thought reminded him that the Noveltys were just a month out from burying their daughter. Their only child.

"We're sorry to pull you away from work at your ranch, Jax, but that's partially why we needed to meet with you today." Frank started right in. No "how've you been," "how's your new place" or even just "you doing okay?"

He'd planned to ask some version of the three. Had run them by Liam just before the baby had fallen asleep in his car seat. The boy was just teetering past newborn, but he had a wisdom in his eyes far beyond Jax's thirty-one years. Or maybe it was just that having a son made Jax that much more conscious of how his every action affected everyone else with whom he came into contact.

"You said you had something to discuss regarding Liam, and anything to do with him always takes precedence over work," Jax told the older man. In another place and time, he might have liked Frank Novelty. Enjoyed his company.

But with the man disapproving of Jax, judging him,

based on one-sided information, he didn't trust his ex-father-in-law even a little bit.

He most certainly didn't look up to him as he had his own father.

Frank and Emma had shared a long glance, one that Jax knew did not bode well for him. Yet he remained seated, outwardly calm, as Frank asked, "Well now, that's not precisely true, is it?" Then without leaving space for Jax to respond said, "In fact, truth is, you leave a helpless, three-month-old infant alone with paid help all day every day, don't you?"

Not every day. And not *all* day. "I stop by the house and check on him several times a day," he told the man. And whenever he was out farther on the ranch, he checked in by video call. He saw Liam. Knew that he was safe and sleeping peacefully. Or being held and content. If he happened to call during a time the little guy was mad, he remained on the line until the diaper change was done, or the formula warmed, and Liam was sucking greedily.

"So you give him what, half an hour, an hour a day at the most?" Frank continued on in his professor-like voice. Making his points with a logic he seemed sure would get him whatever win he was after, not with any hint of aggression.

Christa had adored both of her parents, speaking highly of them from the very first. She'd trusted them to the point that she'd confided in them regarding Jax's lack of ever-lasting love where she was concerned. Had even told them that she'd known he was about to break off their casual three-month fling when she told him she was pregnant.

It didn't seem to matter to them that he'd stood by her, done the right thing and married her. Or that he'd grown to admire her a great deal when he'd seen how dedicated she was to their son. And to them as parents of the child.

Unfortunately, she hadn't been quite as honest with them regarding the man she'd started seeing outside her and Jax's marriage. Nor did Jax ever plan to inform them—or Liam—that she'd been with that man on the boat that had crashed and taken her life the month before.

Jax reminded himself, though, as he chose not to get defensive and respond to Frank's last comment. How many hours a day he spent with his son was not the man's concern. The fact that Liam was healthy, well adjusted and loved was most important.

Frank sat forward then, his hands clasped, elbows on his knees and looked at Jax as he said, "And your lack of attention to this matter just proves the point we intend to make to the judge. You're going to be getting an official notice of the hearing, Jax, but we wanted to tell you in person that we filed a petition with the court to gain legal custody of Liam. We're both healthy, able adults. Neither of us work outside the home anymore. And the child will benefit from having a two-parent family." The older man cleared his throat. "Beyond that, he'll spend his days being raised and taught by doting grandparents who love him, not by paid strangers. Grandparents who raised the mother who adored him, too. We do want you to understand that we'll be as generous with visitation as you'd like. It'll be good for the boy to have regular exposure to your ranch as he grows up."

The boy. Jax's son.

Frank sat back, signaling the end to his perfectly delivered speech.

Burning inside, Jax went still. Breathing deeply to calm

himself. Reminding himself that with their grief so recent neither Emma nor Frank was in their best state of mind.

When he was ready, he quietly said, "I had high hopes when the two of you followed Liam and I as we relocated here to Emerald Ridge, when you found your house, that together we'd provide a solid family support for Liam as he grows up." He started with what he'd have agreed to. The Noveltys having an active participation in Liam's life. "But there is no way I am giving up custody of my son," he stated then, quite clearly. Distinctly. With all the power fatherhood—and growing up with a wealthy, strong dad— had given him. "Most single fathers work during the day," he stated succinctly. "And the majority of them aren't on the premises, available if needed, as I am."

"Oh, you misunderstand if you think we're asking you again for custody, Jax. We already tried that. You weren't willing to compromise," Frank told him, standing, while Emma stayed seated, facing Liam. Her gaze hadn't left the sleeping baby since the conversation had begun. "We're forced to take you to court to do what's best for our grandson. And we're going to use anything we can dig up on you and your family to win, too," he added. "Like the fact that one of the reasons you're working so many hours right now is to undo the damage your stepmother did on the ranch before she was arrested and sent to prison. And another one being that you didn't care enough about your family's ranch to stick around after your father married her. No, other than the four months before Liam was born, and the past three since his birth, you spent the majority of the past two years galivanting around the globe and having casual affairs with young women wherever you landed." Frank paused, glancing down, leaving unsaid that their daughter, Christa, had been among them. Then with a bit of accusation in his gaze said, "Leaving a string of broken hearts behind you. Which fits right in with the rather distasteful Wellington reputation we've been hearing about ever since we arrived in town. Seems it wasn't just your recent stepmother who brought the family down. Your own father married three women, the most recent being twenty-five years younger than him, and a criminal at that. He married her only a year after his second wife died."

Again, Jax bit back the retort that flew to his tongue. His father had buried two wives. One from a car accident that had absolutely nothing to do with him. And the second, after twenty years of marriage, when Jax and his sister Annelise's mother, had died of cancer. But Jax didn't completely disagree with Frank's assessment, either. Although his mother and father's marriage had lasted, he couldn't say a lot for the relationship they'd shared. And it had been a slap in the face to him and Annelise when their father had remarried so quickly after their mother's death, too.

All of which had soured Jax on marriage, but had nothing to do with his ability to raise his son single-handedly. Just because a man didn't excel in the romance department didn't mean he couldn't love deeply. And well. Jax's father might have lacked as a husband, but he'd been a great dad.

"You think degrading Liam's birthright is good for him? Being supportive of him?" He asked the words as much out of curiosity as an attempt to get the Noveltys to see reason.

Emma turned slightly toward him, her hand on the stroller as she looked up at him. "That's just it, Jax. We don't want to have to do any of that. Which is why we're hoping you'll sign over custody of Liam to us. Frank's approach is a bit...gruff...but we really would like to work with you as opposed to against you. We just need you to see that our way is best for Liam. You'll see him as much as you want to, can work as much as you need to and Liam will be loved and adored by his family every minute of the day. Simply put, we have the time, you don't." She sighed softly. "And surely you'll agree that as his grandparents, we have more right to him than a stranger you pay." Her eyes glistened with tears and she said, "All we want to do is love him."

Jax didn't doubt Frank and Emma's adoration for their grandson. He did, however, worry about their ability to present him in a positive light to his son. None of which mattered to the moment at hand.

The most important thing right then was to stress that it was best for Liam if they could all get along and provide him with a cohesive loving environment. Jax tried again. "I want you to have plenty of opportunity to love him. This past month has admittedly been busy with me settling back in at the ranch and you two buying a new home and getting moved in. You haven't had as much time with Liam as you'd like. But that will change going forward. You're welcome at the ranch. Come see him during the day as often as you'd like. But he's *my* son. He lives with me."

Emma glanced at her husband, and stood up beside him as Frank said, "We'll see about that. We'd hoped you'd be reasonable, but it appears that's not the case."

Taking hold of the stroller with both hands, Jax stood, too. "I'm begging you to reconsider, Frank. Emma." He turned his gaze onto each of them individually. "Christa chose to marry me, to live with me, in spite of everything you say about me. It was her choice that I will be the one to continue raising our son. For her sake, don't do this. Honor her wishes."

He might have felt dirty, pulling out all the stops, but he spoke the complete truth. And would do whatever it took to protect his son. To keep Liam at home with the one parent he had left. To raise him with the heritage into which he'd been born.

And when Annelise returned from her trip overseas and married Drake Fortune, Liam's family would grow exponentially. He'd have cousins—including little Joey who, according to Annelise, had been left on the Fortunes' doorstep and adopted by Poppy Fortune and her fiancé, Leo Leonetti. A man Jax had known his entire life. They were great people.

And would be role models for Liam, too.

Emma and Frank shared a long glance. Then, putting her arm through her husband's, Emma turned her back on Jax as Frank said, "You're making a mistake, Jax. We'll see you in court." And the two marched off, backs straight and heads held high.

Priscilla Fortune could hardly believe what she'd just witnessed. Trapped behind a group of trees just to the right of the bench upon which Jax Wellington had been sitting, she held on to the three leashes in her fist as her charges—all rescue animals from the local shelter— sniffed incessantly to find places to do their business.

Three years older than her, Jax had been a regular fixture in the crowd of teenagers from wealthy families who congregated in Emerald Ridge during the summer. Priscilla had been a summer visitor. He'd been a year-round resident, which had given him a lot more clout.

She'd watched him from afar.

But had gotten to know him better in the month she'd been back in Emerald Ridge—her second visit that summer—though prior to that it had been several years since she'd set foot there. She'd made a stop at her cabin on the estate in July to spend a few days with an old friend, and had heard that Jax had left town a couple of years before, after his father's third marriage, and hadn't been back since.

Priscilla had thought that July stopover would be her only visit that summer. Until a mandatory family meeting called by the uncle who'd raised her and her three older siblings along with being a single father to his own daughter, had brought her back the first week of August. Everyone had been called to the summer estate her parents had purchased in Emerald Ridge shortly after they'd been married. The property was originally comprised of a mansion and many acres on the river. To which, with each child born, they'd added a cabin—a McMansion by most standards—in the hopes that as their children grew to adulthood, they would bring their own families home to the ranch whenever they could. Priscilla and her siblings were supposed to have been there just for a few days to commemorate a difficult anniversary—twenty years since their parents had been killed in a plane crash—and to try to find the surprise their parents had told them they'd intended to share with their children upon their return. But those days had morphed into weeks and they were all still there that first week in September.

They'd all searched endlessly over the years for whatever present their parents had for them, to no avail, but with the anniversary upon them, they'd decided they had to make finding the gift a priority for all of them. Their uncle, and their cousin, Uncle Sander's daughter, Kelsey, who'd lived in the main house after Mark and Marlene had passed away, were with them.

But before they'd even had a chance to start looking for any hidden treasure, they'd arrived at the estate only to learn the horrible news that there'd been a murder the previous night. Linc Banning, the son of the Fortune family housekeeper who'd grown up with them in the home they'd all shared, had been shot in the chest and left in the river.

No way Priscilla could just leave, without knowing what had happened to Linc—and why. Her siblings had all hung around as well, and Priscilla, being the helper that she was, had made the rounds in town to find out where her volunteer hours could be put to best use.

One of the places she'd landed had been the animal shelter. Right when Jax was showing up in town with a newborn son, to take over his family's ranch. She'd heard he was asking around for a couple of purebred dogs for the barns, and had suggested, instead, that he rescue a couple of her charges. She'd even delivered them to Jax, for a test run, to help convince him.

And there she stood, hiding out like some kind of peeper—entertaining herself with the thoughts running willy-nilly through her head—in an effort not to embarrass the man. All three dogs had peed. Two were lying in the grass. The third was pulling at the leash and starting to whine.

Jax, who was still holding court at her only way out of the park, was going to hear the dog soon. He'd reclaimed his seat on the bench and was staring out at the water like he'd just lost his best friend.

Priscilla couldn't just stand there and let someone hurt all alone.

"Hey," she said, walking up slowly so the dogs didn't disturb the baby's stroller. "I...was pretty much trapped back there." She gave a backward nod. "That was kind of harsh, huh?"

Looking from Priscilla to the dogs, Jax nodded, but said, "Nothing I can't handle."

She didn't doubt that. Mostly. But the man wasn't doing himself any favors, alienating a rich couple with nothing left to lose. And Priscilla didn't like standing over him. Made her self-conscious, though she had no reason to be.

Sitting on the far end of the bench, she said, "Maybe suggest some kind of mediation," she offered. "The courts have specific counselors for that kind of thing."

His glance wasn't friendly, but it wasn't mean, either. "I don't need mediation. Liam is my son. They have no grounds to take him from me."

"You do know about grandparent rights, yes?" she asked. "In Texas, if the biological grandparent of a deceased parent wants possession of the child, they have some means by which to access that. As long as the other parent is still alive, and there isn't an active adoption case in process. I mean, I'm not a lawyer, but that's the gist of it."

He was staring at her. "How do you know that?"

"I volunteer at a large family law practice in Dallas— hosting seminars for families, acting as a supervisor for visitations when needed…" She stopped, then added, "I have a degree in human relations, and am a certified visitation supervisor. I just don't charge for my services."

"So you're telling me that if the Noveltys present a good enough case showing that it's in Liam's best interests to be with them, instead of me, they could win?"

"It's possible," she told him. "You're looking at judges with leeway to assess situations and make a final decision. More likely, though, you'd be put in mediation that could end up producing some kind of custodial agreement allowing them to care for Liam during the day, or granting them regular visitation rights, similar to what divorced parents get. Meaning they could get him one night a week, and every other weekend, or some such."

He was staring at her, mouth open, as she continued, "Add in their wealth, and yours, and what you're likely to have is a long drawn out battle with expensive lawyers digging up all the dirt they can find to force the other party to relent."

She didn't know the Noveltys, but she'd bet that they were squeaky clean compared to the Wellingtons. Most particularly since the home Jax was raising his son in had recently been a crime scene. Resulting in the legal occupant, and, until recently, part owner of the ranch—Jax's stepmother, Courtney Wellington—being sent to prison.

To make matters worse, the woman had been involved with illegally gained adoption records, and bribing officials to pass off a baby as belonging to another woman. A baby that was not much older than Liam, and had been born in secret on Jax's ranch.

"At some point, the one who keeps fighting the longest will appear to not be working in the best interests of the child," Jax said then, glancing over at her, his expression glum.

"Or they'll seem to be that determined to do whatever it takes to protect the child's interests," she countered, feeling her heart bump a little harder as she watched him. In jeans, cowboy boots and a short-sleeved polo shirt, the dark haired man would turn heads even if he wasn't wealthy.

He'd turned hers a time or two. At the moment, however, she just hurt for him. He'd lost so much in the past few years. His mother. Then a year later his father remarried—jeopardizing his relationships with his kids. And maybe his reputation a bit, too. The next year, he died. At the same time that Jax's family name was being dragged through the mud, his wife was killed, leaving him with an infant son to bring home to the Fortune ranch his step-mother had sabotaged by arranging to have valuable horses stolen and property vandalized.

For one who'd been gravitating to every underdog fight in her path for her entire life, Priscilla was having a hard time separating herself from Jax and his current situation.

As though he'd read her mind, Jax looked from her to Liam, and with his gaze still pointing at his sleeping baby said, "I never saw myself being a father. Or getting married, either. My relationship with Christa, Liam's mom, was just a fling—on both sides. We'd only known each other a few months. But we weren't exclusive. Her choice as much as mine. We had fun together, but didn't see it going anywhere beyond that. Which is partially why it worked."

He paused, and she kept her focus open-eyed and on him. Feeling the heart he was exposing to her. For a man like Jax to be confiding in her meant he was in a pretty desperate state.

"It had pretty much played out its course, we were finding less and less to say to each other, when she turned up pregnant." He shook his head, looking from the baby to Priscilla as he said, "We used protection. Every single time. Not that there were that many of them." Shrugging, he looked back to Liam.

"I'd been ready to head out to another town, embark on my next challenge, but when I found out she was pregnant—she'd insisted on having a paternity test done—I couldn't walk away. Not from my child."

The child had changed the man. Made total sense to her.

Shaking her head, her heart filling with compassion for Jax, Priscilla blurted, "If only you could get someone to act like your fiancée. It'd be a way to show the court that you're serious about family, and that Liam will have a stepmom teaching him, adoring him, one who can be with him during the day." She'd been trying to lighten the moment, but had spoken without thinking. Her biggest fault. One she'd been getting more and more under control.

But the man…he'd been pulling things out of her ever since she'd been back.

Of course, in her own mind, things made a different kind of sense than they sounded out loud. Burning up with embarrassment, knowing her face had to be turning red, she opened her mouth to clean up her mess and blurted, "Before you get the wrong idea, I'm not suggesting that person be me. I was jesting, not being serious. I'm not hitting on you here." Which drew his gaze back to her.

With a hint of a crooked smile that tugged at her some more.

"Not that you aren't one of the town's biggest catches,"

she said. "You are. I'm just…no one is…for rent. I'll shut up now."

His gaze had a new light in it. Which could be good. For him. She'd given him a moment away from his baggage. But she'd only made more of a fool of herself.

"Not that I'd suit this situation, anyway," the words continued to tumble out of her in a pressing attempt to convince him that she had in no way been referring to herself. Because, for a second there, maybe she had been doing so. Which was ludicrous. "I mean, my own reputation…this summer here, with Linc… I'm sure you've heard about that…"

Was it actually possible to die of embarrassment? From self-inflicted humiliation, no less.

Jax was glancing back at Liam, probably trying to ease her disgrace as much he could do, with her being the one inflicting the ignominy on herself. Without turning his head from is child, he said, "I know he was found dead a day or so after I got home. And that he'd approached a man about selling the man his adoption records."

She nodded. Still in disbelief over it all. And eager to change the subject, too. "I went out with him a couple of months ago." She filled him in on the rest of the story. If she didn't, someone else would at some point. "And was dumped by him, too." With no explanation whatsoever. Not that she pointed that part out. Her words had brought his gaze straight to her. He was studying her, open-mouthed. Like she was some kind of bug under a microscope. She just couldn't figure out if he was appalled, amused, or just wishing himself elsewhere.

Leaving her to further lament her bizarre behavior. She'd never found a life calling. Just volunteered all over the land. As the baby of her family, one who'd had to grow up without parents, she'd learned young to deal with life by just keeping herself busy with helping where help was needed. She was a floater. And had just sailed a little too far into Jax's waters.

He still wasn't talking, the silence pressed on her, bringing awkward to new levels. Did she just duck away?

And avoid him in the small circle in which they ran?

"Anyway," she said, "I hope you get an attorney who won't stop until you've won, if you do have to go to court. Ever since I first heard about your situation with Liam and then saw him when I brought the dogs out—I…felt a bond with him. I lost both of my parents to a plane crash. And the cousin I was raised with, she lost her mom in a crash. It just feels right, somehow…purposeful…and important that this child who also lost a mother has a father as dedicated as you are to be there for him. And, seriously, if there's anything I can do to help, feel free to reach out. My uncle was there for me and my siblings, and I'd like to pay that forward if I could." The thought was brand-new to her. And rang with more truth than anything that had hit her in a really long time.

Jax blinked. He was watching her. Still giving no indication whatsoever what he thought about her embarrassing attempt to make it clear that she was not the least bit interested in him.

When, in truth, she was afraid that maybe she was.

Just a little.

Chapter Two

Jax liked Priscilla. The first time he'd noticed her, fifteen or so years before, they'd been at one of the many private shindigs attended by Emerald Ridge's wealthy teenage crowd. It had been a Fourth of July pool party, and she'd witnessed a year-round resident jerk—not Jax—making fun of a less popular, younger summer visitor who wouldn't go off the diving board into the deep end of the pool.

Petite little Priscilla, who was a good three or four years younger than Jerk, had stuck her nose right up to him and asked him if he'd like to step out in front of a moving car, because that's how it felt for some people to jump into deep water. She'd known, though the rest of them hadn't, that the picked on kid had nearly drowned as a toddler, and while he could swim, he'd been drinking and wasn't going to chance a flashback.

Jax had heard that part later. From one of the Fortune cousins who were also year-round residents, unlike Priscilla.

Hating that that young spitfire was standing there embarrassing herself, even as he was grateful to her for distracting him from the hell into which he'd been sinking, he said, "I appreciate the offer. And while I think my boy and I are doing just fine, and I will most definitely be finding the best family attorney in the country. I have to say, I'm just a little bit disappointed that you weren't hitting on me." He grinned. And then said, "I hope your lack of interest doesn't mean that you're going to avoid me at all costs in the future?"

Their circle was small enough that they were bound to meet up. He'd like to know that he had a friend. Even a remote one. He glanced at the stroller as he spoke, to keep his question light and easy. And lost his train of thought as he saw his son's brown eyes gazing up at him.

Eyes just like his own. Priscilla stood, Jax figured to take her leave and remove them both from the hugely uncomfortable morning—to pretend it had never happened, but still be able to smile and say hello if the occasion arose—and then saw her perfectly manicured toes shining bright red outside the bling-covered expensive leather flip-flops. She was standing at the side of the stroller.

The leashed dogs had risen from their resting places in the grass to accompany her. Two of them were small, no more than ten pounds or so. The third, some kind of cocker spaniel mix was tall enough to stick his nose over the side of the stroller.

Jax saw Priscilla grab the dog's collar, in addition to tightening her hold on all three leashes. Then, as he glanced back to his son, was kind of mesmerized, watching the dog and infant staring at each other. Almost as though they were having a conversation. Speaking some language of their own.

The dog wagged its tail. Opened its mouth and started to pant, as though wanting to play.

And… Liam let out a loud sound Jax had never heard before. He gaped at his son.

"He just laughed!" Priscilla exclaimed, and Jax's gaze shot to her face. Noting the delight written all over her expression, but still kind of in shock, too.

Turning his focus back on Liam, Jax watched as the baby wriggled both arms and legs all at once, as though trying to get himself to the dog he was fixated on, and then let out another loud spurt of glee.

"He laughed," he said, feeling as though he'd just witnessed a real miracle. "He's never done that before."

Kneeling beside the stroller, Priscilla said, "It's an omen. He wants his father to fight for him. Wants to stay with you."

And Jax's heart filled with gratitude toward the woman.

Jax stood up. He only had a minute or two before Liam would start to fuss. The boy wanted a clean dry diaper at all times—and was not happy about having them changed—and then he'd want to eat. Two hours was a long time for a little growing guy like him to go without nourishment, and it had already been three.

"I hope you're right," he told Priscilla, and, completely out of character added, "Without my needing to troll for a fake fiancé to rent. After seeing my father's relationships, and just starting the cleanup process from his most recent disaster, I'm not only not a fan of marriage, but pretty much see it as a death knell."

And when he should have left it at that, added, "It's more than just that, though." Still reeling from the meeting he'd just endured with the Noveltys—the news that they'd already filed papers to take his son from him, he continued to stand there, talking. To have someone to talk to. "When Christa was killed in that boating accident, she wasn't alone," he told her. "I first suspected she was stepping out on me within a month of our marriage. She was almost seven months along. I haven't told the Noveltys, or anyone else, and never intend for my son to find out, either." He blew out a ragged breath. "She'd taken back up with a man she'd been in a serious relationship with the year before she met me. And continued the relationship after the baby's birth. She'd told me about him when we were a thing. He was her one true love, and she didn't want to mislead me into thinking that we were anything more than a casual fling. Unfortunately, she was already tied to me when he apparently realized she was his one and only as well. Or maybe he hadn't, and she just didn't have the strength to stay away from him. She wanted to have her cake and eat it, too." He shook his head. "I'll never know, or understand. What I do know is that she was with him when she died. He was killed as well."

Frowning, Jax met Priscilla's gaze. "Please, please keep her stepping out just between the two of us. The Noveltys and Liam can both be hurt by the information. And Lord knows I don't need any more bad gossip following me around, either."

Hazel eyes wide, Priscilla shook her head. Meeting his gaze head-on, she promised, "Of course I won't say anything, Jax. I'm a good person. Really."

He nodded, then gave her a lopsided smile. One that held regret as well as fondness. "I do know that about you."

She nodded. Glanced down at her dogs, loosened their leashes as though preparing to allow them to lead her back to their temporary home. With a chuckle that held a strange kind of commiserate humor, she said, "Just remember I'm here if you need anything. And, just so you know, I'm already contemplating moving to Emerald Ridge full time. Just in case you ever need to reach out. You know, a character witness in court or something. There's nothing in Dallas calling me back, and I've grown accustomed to having my own cottage on the river. A home I'm the boss of. It's kind of nice."

She smiled then, and the warmth in her eyes hit him in the gut.

A sensation he was pretty sure he wasn't going to forget.

Over the next couple of days, Priscilla walked dogs, read to patients in the small private Emerald Ridge Hospital and continued to search for the elusive gift her parents had said they had waiting at the estate for their kids when they got home from the trip from which they'd never returned.

She tried *not* to think about Jax. Or Linc, either.

But found herself remembering Liam's laugh repeatedly at odd times—over her morning tea, or an afternoon walk with a frisky Golden retriever. And thinking of her eldest brother, Roth, who'd just become engaged to Antonia Leonetti, the CFO of Leonetti Vineyards, and was already sharing the parenting of her one-year-old daughter, Georgie. The first time she'd seen Roth holding that young toddler on his hip, Priscilla had felt an unfamiliar longing within herself.

Maybe the first stirrings of motherhood?

She didn't want the rest of the package—the being in love with the father part.

Or maybe it had been the impetus she needed to think outside her own box. She didn't have to be married to adopt a child. Her cousin had just adopted little Joey, and he was adorable. Yeah, Poppy had fallen in love, too, and was now engaged to Leo Leonetti, the CEO of Leonetti Vineyards, but that had happened separate and apart from the baby. She'd already been fostering Joey at that point.

So she should check into local foster parenting. With her visitation supervisor clearance, and ability to provide for a child, she should quickly pass all certification qualifications.

Heading to the computer desk set up in the library of her mini mansion cottage, Priscilla dove into a search, which led to an organization, which led to forms to fill out.

She could foster with the intent to adopt.

And wanted an infant, up to a year old.

Was she being selfish there? What about older kids who needed to be loved? As she'd been when her parents had been killed?

She changed her preferences.

And went to get herself some lunch. In town. She'd learned long ago—and had just had the fact brought home hard by Jax Wellington two days before—that while she had to let her heart lead her, she couldn't just jump every time it ached. People got hurt that way. Most particularly by someone who offered to do something, and then, no matter how hard she'd tried, had had an inability to follow through in the end.

As her first volunteering stints in high school had taught her. She'd signed up to be a mentor with a local youth organization. And hadn't realized that her school commitments prevented her from being available when her little sister had tragedy strike in the middle of the day, for one.

She had to take time. To let her heart and mind process her choice. And then she could hit send to get the ball rolling on becoming a mother.

It felt good. And got her mind off the gorgeous rancher with the motherless baby who'd been on her mind far too much since her unexpected meeting with Jax Wellington in the park on Monday.

Dressed in her favorite purple skirt, fluttery short-sleeved top and another of her plethora of expensive flip-flops with bling, she treated herself to Captain's, the penthouse seafood restaurant in the Emerald Ridge Hotel. Because she wanted the peacefulness of the view. And poached salmon.

She'd had that fish all over the world, but nothing held up to Captain's. Possibly because salmon at Captain's had been the last meal she'd shared with her mom and dad.

It felt fitting to be there again—remembering herself back then, feeling their adoration, bringing back the memory with some taste association—as she contemplated the next phase of her life.

Maybe it was Linc's death, or her eldest brother finally settling down, but Priscilla's life was feeling empty with only volunteering to fill it up. She needed more. Real commitment. The kind that you had to meet even when you didn't feel well.

The kind you *wanted* to meet no matter how sick you were.

She'd just paid her bill and was sitting there in her secluded little corner for one, finishing her glass of iced tea, when her phone buzzed a call.

The number was local. Not in her contacts.

Keeping her voice as low as she would were she speaking to someone at her table, she answered. "Hello?" Perhaps it was someone at the shelter, or the hospital could need her.

"Priscilla?" Her heart lurched, and her stomach grabbed hold of the salmon she'd just sent its way. She knew the voice.

"Jax?" she said, giving herself away before it dawned on her that it made her look like some kind of stalker— knowing who he was during their first phone call together.

How embarrassing…

"Yeah, listen, I'm sorry to bother you, but I was wondering if you have any time free today?"

Her heart lurched, even as she cursed a fate that conjured up the man just when she was turning her thoughts away from him. He was asking her out? He was asking her out!

No. Wait.

The dogs.

Or he needed a babysitter.

Thoughts flew…and landed. "Of course, what do you need?" she asked. One of the canines she'd left wasn't working out, or he needed another one.

"A chance to talk to you," he said, sounding oddly out of sorts. "Any way you could head out to the Wellington Ranch?"

"When?" Like it mattered? She had the rest of the day. Just needed time to hit send on the foster/adoption application.

"Whatever works for you. I'll meet you at the house anytime you say."

Curious.

And very interesting.

"How about twenty minutes from now?" she asked, not caring a whole lot if she sounded eager. He'd called. And Captains was halfway between home and his ranch. Why waste gas and pollute the environment further by making the trip into town twice? But just to make sure he understood that she wasn't…as eager as she was…she added, "I've just finished lunch at Captain's and can head your way before going home."

Lunch at Captain's. Kind of implied that she was with someone. Maybe even a date. After all, the place was popular for first dates and special occasions.

The latter of which she'd been having—just not with anyone still living.

And yet, as Priscilla hung up and headed out, she felt more alive than she had in a very long time.

Jax paced the huge foyer in the mansion where he'd grown up. The grand staircase just behind it would have been a better place to expend his over-the-top nervous energy.

Up until the moment he'd found out he was going to be a father, Jax was pretty certain he'd never had a neurotic moment in his life. Since then, they'd just kept coming.

Some were justified. Like his current predicament. He should never have said a word to the Noveltys until he'd spoken with Priscilla.

Her reputation was at stake and the Fortune clan's standing in town was much more valuable than Jax's had ever been. They actually had something honorable to uphold.

His family had been the lesser wealthy of the two, though not by much, and the lesser respected as evidenced by the century old feud between the families. A Fortune had left a Wellington bride at the altar and then rubbed salt in the wound by sending over a skunked bottle of supposed $1000 wine as an apology.

And he'd claimed a Fortune as his own without her knowledge. What in the hell had he been thinking?

Priscilla drove up in a rather sedate, blue luxury sedan and Jax pulled open the door. Looking overeager was the least of his problems.

Lying to the couple trying to take his son away from him in order to get them to drop their court case had been just about the least intelligent thing he'd ever done.

But then, other than when his mother had been dying and he'd been unable to console himself, let alone Annelise, he'd never felt so desperate before.

Still in the suit he'd worn to the courthouse in town, Jax met Priscilla at her car. Holding the door open for her and barely backing up enough to give her room to get out.

Frowning, she locked gazes with him, their faces only inches apart over the top of the door frame that separated them as she stood. "Jax? What's wrong? Is it Liam…?"

"He's fine." Jax practically hissed the words through breathlessness. And then, backing up, giving her room, said, "He's asleep upstairs in the nursery. His nanny is watching him so that we can talk," he assured her.

"Then…what is it?"

"I did a really stupid thing, Priscilla, and I'm sorry." He looked her in the eye as he apologized. And stood straight, right in front of her, hands at his sides as he confessed all. "I had a meeting with my lawyer this morning regarding the Novelty's filing. We'd planned to go to court to meet with the judge, hoping to be able to get the case thrown out of court. But it turned out that not only is the case *not* being thrown out, it's been moved up. To the beginning of next week. Something about there being enough doubt as to the appropriateness of an infant being solely in my care when, until he was born, I've been moving from place to place as the spirit took me and have never even had a long-term relationship..."

His tongue practically tumbled over his teeth as he tried to get the words out as rapidly as possible. As though by doing so he could somehow divert the disaster he'd created.

Out of something she'd said in jest, and then had backtracked from so far she'd run herself over. The woman couldn't have made it more clear she'd been talking in jest. Only a very selfish man would even pretend not to have known that. Or a desperate one.

"My lawyer was seriously concerned that they'd be awarded at least shared custody," he said. "Which means I couldn't make any decisions regarding his life, medically or otherwise, without their cooperation. I panicked, Priscilla."

Her hazel eyes wide and filled with compassion, she said, "Oh my God, Jax! Surely the judge didn't rule already? Without even giving you a chance to be heard?"

Shaking his head, he told her, "It's far worse than that."

Eyes wide and worried, she asked, "They got full custody? You said he's upstairs. Have you been given an amount of time to turn him over?"

"I picked up the phone, right there in my lawyer's office, got Emma and Frank on the line and told them that I hadn't wanted to say anything before, out of respect for the fact that their daughter, *my wife*, had just died recently. But that since returning to Emerald Ridge, I'd reconnected with someone from my past, and that we've been seeing each other every day for most of the past month." He cleared his throat. "And that I, uh, wanted to propose, but was afraid how it would appear to them..."

Mouth open, she stared at him. "You've been seeing someone?"

She'd paled.

"No!" he said too loudly. She looked at him.

Studied him, was more like it. Clearly concerned. And also perplexed.

Just wait, he wanted to warn her. Was trying to avoid telling her the next part, even knowing it was his entire reason for having called her in the first place.

To warn her.

Putting his hands in his pockets, he said, "Frank and Emma wanted to know who she was. They wanted a name."

She nodded. Clearly waiting for him to get to his point.

And he said, "I gave them yours."

Chapter Three

Standing on that paved, circular driveway, Priscilla cataloged the fog in her brain. The weightlessness of her limbs. Felt cold and hot at the same time. And numb. Blessedly numb.

"You…what?" she gasped softly.

Pulling his hands out of the pockets of his pants, Jax wrung them together. "I know," he said, hanging his head for a second, before looking her in the eye again. "I'm so sorry. None of it was preplanned. Or given a single thought, for that matter. I panicked. I picked up the phone, and I started talking. Everything you'd said Monday in the park, all that about your certification, and knowing the system, about what you thought might work…it was hitting me like a ton of bricks, and then your opinion of the only way out for me—faking a fiancée, it just came pouring out. Then they asked for a name and you were the only person on my mind. I know you were just kidding Priscilla. I'll take care of this. I just needed to warn you. I know how stuff travels around here and I didn't want you to think I was mocking what had obviously been said in jest."

She heard his words. Understood them. Still felt as though she was in a cocoon of cotton that couldn't touch her. That she was watching a pretty sophisticated fabrication, not living real moments in her life.

Was a situation still just make-believe when a look in a guy's eyes reached inside and tugged at your heartstrings?

"You gave them my name." She repeated his sentence just to hear him say she'd misunderstood him.

When he nodded, she felt another little spark inside. One that left her feeling...weak. Vulnerable. And kind of intrigued, too.

They'd never even been out in a small group together, let alone on a date.

He spread his arms wide, his gaze looking lost, and shaking his head said, "I'll take care of it, Priscilla. Like I said, in those seconds, the reality of losing my son... I just panicked. Said the only thing that came to mind. I'm so sorry I put you in this position. I've already left them a voicemail, asking them to call me back at their earliest convenience so I can tell them the truth."

He'd told his son's grandparents that he was engaged to her. The whole thing was so farfetched, all she could do was stand there and...not mind that he'd used her name that way.

"I was desperate," he repeated while she struggled to find a response appropriate to the situation.

When all she could think was that his situation *was* desperate.

And...he'd left them a voicemail to tell them the truth. Was apologizing for using her name.

As though that was the issue. And it hit her. "What did they say? When you told them you wanted to marry me?"

"'That lovely young woman visited mean old Uncle Edrick when he was here a couple of weeks ago to see our new home and had ended up in the hospital. She'd read to him when no one else could stand his cranky ways.'" He mimicked every word. Having heard Emma Novelty Monday morning, Priscilla could almost hear the woman saying them.

And for a second, felt kind of pleased with herself, too. It was nice to know that her volunteering really made an impact. And helped families as well as patients.

She was gearing up to say as much to Jax, when his gaze grew serious and bore straight into her. "They said that if I marry you, a clearly loving soul and caretaker who comes from a great family, they'll pull the petition. *For now.*"

Oh. Her mouth dropped open. Not a word came out. Right. Other times, like Monday in the park, they couldn't wait to escape and embarrass her, but the one time she needed them…

"They then added that I better be sure I love this one. And that if the marriage doesn't work out, they'll reinstate the petition with another point of reference to add to their case."

She felt the jab they'd taken at Jax even if he hadn't. "What'd you tell them?" she asked, letting curiosity continue to rule the moment for her. Keeping it about him. His predicament. What he'd done. Not on the fact that she, strangely, wasn't affronted by the entire outlandish situation. He'd said he was going to take care of it. Had already left them a voicemail.

"I assured them that you and I are a perfect love match." Her heart stuttered in her chest until he said, "Which is true given our mutual disillusionment with love."

Right. Heart beating again, Priscilla liked that what

he'd told them was true. Seemed to bode well. For what, she wasn't quite sure.

Wasn't going there, yet.

But she was getting closer.

A lot closer.

Depending on what he said or did next.

"So I guess, since you're still here and not throwing things at me, that we can still nod and say hello when we run into each other now and then?"

She smiled then. "Of course," she said. But her expression clouded up almost immediately. "Seriously Jax, what are you going to do?"

He shrugged. "As far as I can see I have two options. One is to figure out how I possibly give up my son, at least partially." Yet the look of pain that crossed his face told her that this was impossible for him to consider, realistically.

Which left only...

"And the other?" she asked, holding her breath, chest tight with the need to know his second option. Hanging all her hope that it was better than the first.

"Ask you if your offer to do anything you can to help was legitimate, and if so, if it still stands."

"Of course. How can I help?" The Noveltys held her in high esteem. Maybe if she talked to them about Jax.

"Pretend to be my fiancée. Which, based on the Noveltys argument that family should be raising Liam, would mean you moving in here. And would involve a fake marriage, too, until it no longer suits."

Priscilla's mouth dropped open. She had to tell him no. Of course. But, considering how upset he already was, understandably so, she had to find the right words. They didn't come. A strong sense of something meaning more than logic did. A way her life could be of real purpose. And a heart that was suddenly more engaged than it had ever been. As though her parents were nudging her. Jax had touched parts of her heart that no one else had ever reached. His predicament, that motherless little boy, her sudden longing to be a mother. It was all ganging up on her. The idea that her mother would understand brought a curious kind of acceptance inside her. So she held out her hand.

"What's that for?" he asked, watching her sideways palm as though he wasn't sure whether or not she was getting ready to slap him with it.

"In my world it's customary to shake on the most important deals," she told him.

And nearly melted into a puddle when she saw the flood of gratitude that filled his eyes.

Jax wasn't sure what he was supposed to do next. Start talking practicalities. Lock in the details. Or grab up Priscilla Fortune and hug her to him, showering her with the affection he suddenly felt for her. The utter amazement that someone, anyone, would do something so incredibly huge, for him.

And for Liam. He knew his son was the real reason she'd agreed to help them. The second Priscilla had looked at Liam sleeping in his stroller the other day, her entire being had softened.

He hadn't really thought about it, consciously, since. But figured that the realization had lingered, rising up to push him to action that morning in his lawyer's office.

And thinking of which…

He took the hand Priscilla had proffered. Held on to it. Shook it. Then put his other hand atop it. Still holding on. "Are you sure?" he asked. "You'd be giving up your life…" While he'd be gaining his.

The mansion they'd be sharing was huge. Other than in matters to do with Liam, they never even had to see each other. He'd keep the night shift. She'd have the day.

Priscilla put her other hand on the pile between them. "I'm sure," she told him. She was looking him right in the eye. Her voice was steady. "And I'm not giving up my life, Jax. To the contrary, I've found a purpose for it. I don't believe in love any more than you do. Not for me. Like you, I've never been in a serious relationship. And have recently been thinking about adopting or fostering a child. So, in a weird way, this kind of makes sense. I'm standing here curiously excited about it. And feel happier than I can remember feeling in a while. It'll involve a move, yes, but my cottage is mine forever, whether I'm living in it or not. And…" She looked behind him, nodded toward the huge mansion in which he'd grown up, and said, "Judging by the outside, and what I've heard of this place, it's as nice or nicer than our family home in Dallas."

The smile on her face tantalized him, and he leaned forward, placing his lips on hers.

The kiss wasn't meant to be sexy. It was a soft, heartfelt thank you. That lingered a bit too long.

When he pulled away, Priscilla looked a bit surprised for a second. Until she blinked. Nodded. Then disentangled her hands and pulled her phone out of the back pocket of her skirt.

Drawing his gaze in that direction, and lower, to the perfectly shaped long legs that the hemline left exposed.

Did marriages arranged for purposes other than love still involve the fringe benefits? He'd marry her, either way. If celibacy was what it took for him to have all legal rights to his son, he'd still sign on for life.

"There's a three-day—seventy-two hour, to be exact—waiting period from the time you apply for a marriage license until you can get married," Priscilla said, tending to the practical matters that should have been first and foremost on Jax's mind. "You told the Noveltys that you were going to propose to me, but that doesn't mean we have to have the wedding overnight."

She was miles ahead of him.

Shoving his hands in the pockets of his suit pants, Jax tried to ignore the sensations running rampant through his body, and corralled his brain. They had business to take care of.

"What do you think about moving in here? I'll get the ring, we can tell our families about the engagement, then give ourselves a week or two to settle in. You're a Fortune. Your family's going to be expecting a big wedding…"

Her face lost its glow as she shook her head. "I can't do that, Jax. No way I'm going through all the rigama-role of formal nuptials. I wouldn't want that even if I was marrying for real. For love."

She didn't want one day that was all about her? The woman was unlike any he'd ever met before.

Before he pulled himself out of the muck of feelings that were popping up all over inside him, *distracting* him, Priscilla said, "I mean, if you need that, or think that it's important, I'm not saying I wouldn't be willing to partici-pate, if it's what it takes to secure Liam's future, I just—"

"It's okay," Jax interrupted, grabbing her hand again.

"This is *our* wedding. We can do whatever we want, and if getting the license and marrying three days later at the courthouse pleases you, then that's what we'll do."

The words, the turn his world had taken, were surreal. As was the fact that they were standing there getting engaged, talking about what kind of wedding they'd have, on his driveway. "You want to come inside?" he asked. "Take a look around?"

She smiled up at him, and his heart leaped a bit. And when she threaded her arm through his, walking up the steps to his elegant home, he wondered what he'd gotten himself into.

While knowing that, no matter what it ended up looking like, he was fully on board.

Which in itself was so far outside a normal realm for him that he could only buckle up and hope they all survived the ride.

The massive staircase with its ornate railings immediately invoked visions of kids playing on those carpeted steps, their heads sticking out between the railings to peek down below.

Maybe she'd played on the stairs in the Fortune mansion in Dallas as a kid. She couldn't remember having done so.

While Liam continued to sleep upstairs in the nursery attached to Jax's bedroom suite, Jax showed Priscilla around the huge house. "You could have two families living here without ever running into each other," she said aloud at one point. "Our home is immense, but it always felt like we were bumping into one another..."

"It seemed smaller when Annelise and I were kids," he

told her as he took her to the second wing on the other side of the mansion. "The housekeeper is here regularly, but other than a brief walkthrough, I haven't been in this part of the house since I've been back. It was where Courtney lived. Feel free to do anything you'd like with it."

The words hit her kind of hard. Was he telling her that he didn't expect her to share his and Liam's portion of the home? She was to be exiled in an entire home's worth of space—twice the size of her cottage, which was a mini-mansion in itself—*alone*?

"What about Annelise?" she asked. Jax's sister was engaged, to Priscilla's cousin, but the mansion had always been her home, too. "Maybe she'd like to use the space for something."

Jax shook his head. "Unlike me, she lived here with Courtney. And has no desire to have anything more to do with the place." Courtney Wellington, a wicked stepmother if ever there was one. Hard to believe the woman had done so much damage in just the two years she'd been a Wellington.

Priscilla had no desire to live in the woman's space.

"How about we make it a guest wing?" she suggested, not trying to cause trouble right at the start, but needing to speak up. "I'm here to be a mother to Liam, right? Not just to keep up appearances with your ex-in-laws? I'll be caring for him during the day." And evenings and nights, too, as necessary. She hoped.

A wave of panic passed through Priscilla. She was changing her entire life and didn't even have the most basic of plans in place.

And yet…she was there, walking through the house.

Moreover, she wanted to be there. Was feeling anticipation for the first time in a very long while.

"You want to stay in my wing." Jax had taken too long to respond.

She glanced over at him. "You'd rather I didn't?" Then what was the point of her being there? Her future, foreseeably, was going to involve helping him raise a happy, healthy child. No matter what other pursuits she might take upon herself. Or continue to pursue as time allowed. Philanthropy would always have a place in her life.

When Jax's only answer was to take Priscilla's hand and lead her down the second flight of stairs back to the main foyer, and then, into some kind of library room, she prepared herself to be dismissed.

And if he'd had a different vision of her place in the household, then she should be. She'd thought she'd found a more personal, long-term purpose for her life, in addition to volunteer work and extended family. A new purpose that excited her. That she knew she'd be good at.

But if all he wanted was for her to move in—and then go on living as she had—she'd rather stay in her cottage.

Which left Liam…where?

The whole point of their agreement was to ensure the cohesive future for a three-month-old baby. And she was going to buckle at the first sign of discomfort to herself?

Just because Jax didn't actually want her involved in the daily runnings of his and Liam's lives didn't mean that she couldn't work her way in. Then hopefully, at some point in the future, the little boy would begin seeking her out.

And the nanny? The Noveltys didn't approve of a nanny raising their grandchild.

But nannies were a common part of wealthy families. So as long as there was a wife, who conceivably was present during the day, caring for her child with the help of a nanny, Jax would pass muster?

And was she really so desperate to find a life for herself that she'd settle for being ostracized from the family with which she lived?

Was she really going to risk Liam's future because of her living quarters? Was she *that* selfish?

Jax had taken a seat on a big, brown leather couch. She pulled a rocker over and settled into it. Gliding slowly back and forth. Finding the movement therapeutic.

Sitting forward, his elbows on his knees, hands clasped, as he had the other day in the park, Jax seemed to be studying the toes of his shiny black leather shoes. She waited, needing him to work through whatever was bothering him so she'd know where she stood.

The odd, almost hungry look in his eyes when he finally glanced up at her sent shivers through her. The *good* kind.

Except, in their situation, they weren't good at all.

"There are some practicalities I need to discuss," he began, and any pleasant sensations inside her were replaced with dread.

But she was a Fortune. She knew how to keep up appearances. How to push aside self-interest in order to help others. "I'm listening," she said, keeping her tone even. Expression calm.

Like she was at any one of the huge numbers of functions she'd attended over the years, representing her family's money. Their financial contributions.

Throwing up his hands, he looked right at her and said, "Us. What do we look like?"

She wanted to talk about their outward appearances. The fact that they both presented well.

But knew that if there was any chance of a future she really believed she wanted to work, she had to be all in from the start. "Speaking only for myself, of course," she began, cringing inwardly when she heard herself stating the obvious. "I don't want my husband having affairs. It doesn't reflect well on me, on him, on the family unit and most definitely wouldn't be best for Liam."

Didn't mean him seeing women discreetly would be a deal breaker. Not necessarily. But it would be a reason to slow down and think more about what they were doing.

"How do you feel about wives having affairs?" His question was such a surprise, her head shot up, her gaze straight on him.

"Exactly the same. And if you're asking me if I plan to see other men while we're married, the answer is an unequivocal no. In case you forgot, I have no desire to get romantically involved, which is why this works for me."

Pursing his lips, he nodded. And she discovered that he was just as well versed at keeping up appearances as she was. She had no idea what he was thinking.

Until he said, "So that brings me back to us."

His pointed glance, the slight raise of his eyebrow and the cock of his head suddenly had her warming in places that were usually pretty tepid inside her. He seemed to be waiting for her to respond to his statement.

Her only reaction was to keep her breathing even and wait.

"Do we live platonically? Or not?" Yep. She'd known

that was where he was going. Someplace she should have gone before she'd so quickly agreed to his outlandish second option.

And most particularly before she'd held out her palm for a handshake to seal their deal.

She got his dilemma. She was asking a virile, very good-looking man to live without sex for the foreseeable future.

One who surely had a healthy sexual appetite.

While she hadn't slept with a man in…a couple of years. At least.

Panicking, and a little unusually warm down below, too, she came back to the one thing she knew. She had to be honest. "I think we start out that way," she told him. "With an understanding that if something develops mutually between us, the door is always open."

She'd just agreed to have sex with the man. Clearly, he had interest or they wouldn't be having the conversation.

And her darn body was making her feelings on the matter quite clear to her. Shockingly so.

He sat back and was watching her with an odd light in his eyes. One she couldn't quite decipher. There was admiration there—whether it was sexual or not, she wasn't sure. "Then I'd say we've found the answer to our original conversation," he said.

Drawing a blank, she stared at him. They were discussing getting naked and touching each other. What had come before that?

"You move into my wing with Liam and I," he said, as though they were discussing who was going to plan dinner menus.

Excitement sparked through her—she was more than

just warm down below—and rocked a bit more voraciously on the glider. "So on to other details," she practically blurted. "I'll need an introduction to your housekeeper. And the rest of the staff, obviously. I enjoy meal planning, and that kind of thing, so if you're willing, I'll be happy to take that on. I'll just need your preferences, your likes and dislikes…"

Her words trailed off when his eyes took on a darker, different kind of hungry look.

At which point she realized just how much she wanted to know all about those likes and dislikes, too. Wanted to feel his appetite all over her body.

A brand-new experience for her. Kind of scary, yet utterly exciting at the same time.

Adding a whole other facet to the deal she'd agreed upon.

One that had, in less than hour, taken on a powerful life of its own.

As she sat there, rocking, watching him, Priscilla couldn't help but ponder the possibility of someday wanting to know him in every way a wife knows her husband.

Chapter Four

He couldn't have sex with her. For Jax, sex had to be casual. Always. Only way he could do it. And with Priscilla, it would be bigger. More.

Intense.

Because everything about the woman came from the heart.

Who gave up her own life to raise someone else's baby?

Foregoing the chance to have her own family so he could have his?

And yet, it fit. From what she'd said, and what he'd heard about her from the rumor mill, for Priscilla's whole life, she'd been the one noticing what people needed, and trying to help them attain it.

So who helped her attain her greatest desires?

Couldn't be him. Not if they involved sex.

It would be good between them. Hell, who was he kidding? It would be mind-blowingly fantastic. And then there'd be problems. She'd want more from him, and he'd end up breaking her heart because he just plain didn't have that extra dimension to give.

He could pretend for a while.

But for a lifetime?

No, their relationship had to stay platonic. It was the

only way they'd work long-term. And as bizarre as their plan was, he wanted it to work. Badly.

It was the only way he'd ever have a family. And if things actually flowed into fruition like they both thought they could, she'd have a family of her own, too. An untraditional one, maybe. But family just the same. All legally wrapped up and signed in ink.

If things worked out.

Then, maybe, sometime down the road, she'd want to adopt Liam, too. Become his official mother with all legal rights to him in the event that something happened to Jax.

She'd heard Liam cry as he woke up from his nap— all the way from the library, the tiny sound had reached her. And had insisted that she go up, change him, learn where things were.

She'd fed him, and rocked him back to sleep, too.

While Jax had a conversation with Sasha, his housekeeper who'd happily offered to help with Liam at times when Priscilla had to be elsewhere. After which he let go of the nanny Annalise had helped him find before he even got to town with his son. The dismissal came with a large severance and glowing references.

And that's when it hit Jax that they were really doing it. Going through with the absurd plan. *Getting married.*

It was as though Sasha's seal of approval was more binding than the license they'd yet to apply for. If nothing else, sharing their news, hearing her congratulations, made it all more real.

When Priscilla went home to start packing what she'd want at Jax's place immediately, he drove into town and, still in his suit, went into a store he'd never actually shopped at before. And bought the most exquisite diamond engagement ring. The rows of smaller diamonds that formed an outer circle were all fine and good, but the two-karat diamond—with near perfect clarity—that sat atop the rest spoke of Priscilla to him.

All the bling with nearly blinding bling on top.

The plan to marry a woman he'd never even dated might be ludicrous. But he had little choice. The engagement was the only way he preserved his life with his son.

With the ring in his pocket, Jax went back to his lawyer's office to make changes to his will. Pursuant to any marriage he might enter into with Priscilla Fortune. In the event of his untimely demise, she was to be taken care of for the rest of her life, with rights of occupancy of his ranch until her death. The bulk of his estate would go to Liam, with his wife as executor.

He wasn't going to be able to give her the true intimacy that she might end up craving—or the love she deserved—but he had other things to offer.

As long as she was a part of his and Liam's family, she was to get the benefit of every one of them.

And it would never be enough to pay the debt he owed her.

It didn't take long for Priscilla to load the trunk she'd brought with her from Dallas for what she'd thought was going to be a few days in Emerald Ridge—a week at the most.

The rest of what was in her cottage—including the twenty-four place setting of everyday dishes she'd chosen herself—she could go through more slowly, deciding what to leave there, and what to take to Jax's place.

The dishes were what she wanted most, just because

the pattern made her happy. She'd see about either changing out the ones that Jax had, or adding to them.

Whether she took them with her or not, they'd be accessible to her. The cottage was hers whether she was staying in it or not.

A fact that made moving into Jax's abode far less daunting than it might have been. She wasn't losing her own place. She was merely going to be staying somewhere else.

Not a mindset she could share with the family who thought she'd be vacating the place permanently.

Which was one of the reasons she was at her cottage, packing up, and not making any effort to see her siblings. Or uncle. Or cousin. To the contrary, she wasn't yet ready to go down that road.

She needed time to settle into her new skin enough to convince them that her marriage was a legitimate love match.

Eventually, down the road, if things worked out and the marriage worked well enough for her and Jax to make it a way of life, she'd want to move all of her personal things out of the Fortune Dallas estate, but that was a thought for a future time. If there was something she found she needed before that faraway point caught up to them, she could always make a jaunt to Dallas. Or send for what she wanted.

Eventually. Down the road. If.

She'd made a long-term commitment to marry, and raise a child. There'd been no qualifier to that. No escape hatch.

She went through the drawers in her bedroom, just checking to see if there was anything she'd want right away. Her fingers caught against something hard in the bottom of her nightstand, and she pulled out a book. A journal. Memories assailed her as she opened the cover and saw the date on the inside. The summer she'd been seventeen. Uncle Sander—who'd only been twenty-four when he'd taken on the four Fortune orphans, in addition to raising his own motherless daughter—had let her stay in her cottage alone when they'd visited Emerald Ridge that year. As long as she was present at the family table for every meal.

Priscilla had relished the independence. Had come into her own sense of being during those couple of months. Turning the pages, Priscilla got lost in what had been for a bit. Some entries seemed so distant they were like part of another world. Others brought more memories flooding back.

She'd been dating that summer. Because she'd had one major dream. To have a husband and family of her own. With a mother and a father in the home. Raising their children together. She'd had all the material wealth any kid could ever want, but ever since her parents died, she hadn't had a mother and father to turn to. Setting her curfew. Waiting for her to get home.

Instead, she'd returned to an empty cottage with no one realizing that she was there fifteen minutes before curfew.

Sitting there, feeling the intensity of that dream again, the need that had prompted it, Priscilla hated that the only portion of that fantasy that she was realizing was a sham marriage.

She'd had her future planned that summer. And yet, over the years, she hadn't even come close to fulfilling that wish. She was almost thirty and her life was just passing by.

And then it hit her. The marriage wasn't what she'd once envisioned for herself, but another portion of the dream was. She and Jax were providing a family for a little boy who would be able to grow up in a home with his father. With two parents.

Beyond that, she was emulating the parental figure in her life whom she adored beyond measure. Uncle Sander might not have been mother and father, but he'd done the jobs of both. Raising five kids on his own, all of whom were leading successful, productive lives. Contributing positively to society.

Even the *falling in love* part of her and Jax's story that they were telling to the world held some kernel of truth. Because in the time between one change and feeding, she'd fallen irrevocably in love with little Liam.

And couldn't wait to get back to him.

Or his father.

Putting her journal back in the bottom of the drawer where she'd left it for so long, Priscilla allowed herself to think about the man she was marrying. To contemplate the unexpected feelings that had been cropping up every time she was with him. The ones that had nothing to do with compassion or any kind of charitable act. The physical ones, more powerful than she'd thought possible for her.

But there was more. Like honor. Respect. The man stood up to do the right thing, completely disrupting his entire life plan, to marry a woman just to be able to raise his own child. From what Jax had told her about the union, he hadn't been in love with Christa, but he'd been committed to her.

And he was going that route a second time, too. With Priscilla. Committing to her. Making promises that she hoped and prayed he'd keep. Marriage didn't have to be about romantic love. Sometimes the strongest relationships were based on trust. Respect. Mutual goals.

She wasn't going into the next phase of her life wearing rose-colored glasses, setting herself up for pain. Rather, she was marrying a man she liked and admired, one she'd been attracted to from afar since before she'd written that journal at seventeen. Her feelings for him weren't a lie.

And though they had a secret regarding the marriage— their reason for having one—she was still going into it with a heart full of truth.

With her trunk, and an extra suitcase, in her car, Priscilla went back inside to check the refrigerator for items that would spoil, deciding to leave everything but the most critical ones. She'd be living at the Wellington Ranch, but she could still bring Liam to the Fortune estate during the day as she wished.

The thought brought a plethora of plans tumbling forth, the things she'd need for the baby; a portable crib, changing table and supplies, feeding supplies and baby monitor rushed to the top of the list. And then she stopped. Looked around her, and knew that she had something else that she had to do immediately. If she didn't get with her family right away, it would only be a matter of time before they'd heard the news elsewhere. And they'd be less inclined to buy into the story if she hadn't been excited enough by it to tell them herself. They'd also be hurt. And bringing pain to her loved ones, old and new, was the last thing Priscilla wanted to do. Ever.

Which was why, when she couldn't stall any longer at

her cottage, she drove up to the main house, and seeing her uncle and both of her older brothers standing outside talking, got out and strode up to them.

"I've got news!" she said, calling out before she'd fully reached them.

"I'm engaged!" Had the upcoming union been a love match, it's how she'd have played the moment. So what they'd be expecting. She was the baby sister. The youngest niece.

"You're what?" Roth was frowning as he studied.

"Engaged, Sweetie? For real? To who?" Uncle Sander's question followed right on Roth's tail.

Harris, her suave international businessman brother asked, "How can you be engaged when we didn't even know you were dating anyone?"

Trust Harris to get right to the heart of the matter. Giving her the opening she needed.

"Because I didn't want anyone giving me opinions, judging, or questioning my choice. It's Jax Wellington. And yes, I know what you're going to say, guys. His family is a shambles. His stepmother was just sent to prison, he's a widowed single dad, but it's not as though our family is so perfect, either. And I want this. I want…him." She tried not to think about the hidden truth in that statement as she pushed on. "More than anything I've ever wanted." Her chin lifted as she delivered that last bit.

Miraculously silencing all three men. For a second or two.

"Still," her uncle started in first. "Don't you think it's a little sudden? I mean, why not have him over to dinner? Take time to really get to know him."

Have him over for dinner so they all could grill him, she translated.

"He's only been back in town for a month," Roth pointed out then, as if she wasn't aware of the fact. "And his wife was just killed three months ago. He's likely on the rebound."

Her eyes narrowed, she looked up at Harris. Who said, "It *is* a little soon, Pris. Don't you think?"

Priscilla grit her teeth. Smiled. She had to get out of there before they saw through her. She loved them all so much. Loved how fiercely they'd watched out for her from the second they'd heard about the plane crash that had taken away the two people who'd adored her most.

Thinking of Jax, who'd also lost a parent young, and then his father, and a wife, too, and of little Liam, who was at risk of being taken from the father who adored him, she issued the one truth that came to her.

She was a grown woman. Not a little girl, anymore.

And the Wellington men needed her far more than anyone else ever had.

"When you know, you know," she said.

Then turned her back and walked away.

Jax was at home late Wednesday afternoon, pacing in the midst of keeping himself busy with things he didn't normally do—had never done—like making certain that the linens and towels in the room on the other side of Liam's were fresh.

He studied the walls in both rooms, determining that a door could easily be cut between the two. And made a call to get the work started—and completed—the next day. Which then required a conversation with Sasha regarding the extra cleaning detail that would be needed due to sawdust in the air. A fan in the event of paint fumes.

And he checked the time. *Constantly.* His smart watch was right there, on his wrist. Big and bold and staring up at him.

Past four and the quick trip Priscilla had been going to take out to the Fortune Estate to collect some things had turned into several hours.

Which was creating several completely uncharacteristic dilemmas within him. Had something happened to her? A car accident? No one would know to notify him. Or have any idea that his life would be turned upside down by the news.

Had she changed her mind? The more likely scenario. One for which he couldn't blame her. A possibility that he should actually be preparing for, rather than finalizing orders for a new door where currently there was only a wall.

Another option popped up, but was just as quickly trashed, was that she was just a prevaricator. One who didn't pay attention to time, or people waiting on her, but just floated through life doing her thing on her own schedule.

First, Priscilla had no way of knowing that he was waiting on her. And second, the woman was more aware of others than anyone Jax had ever known. It was like she had a sixth sense where underdogs were concerned.

Not that he *was* one. But the point was valid, making consideration number three moot.

He changed and fed Liam. Tended to a situation brought to him by a couple of ranch hands—assuring them that he'd be out on the fence line by six the next morning—and made reservations at Cucina for two for dinner, asking Sasha to stay with Liam that evening in exchange for the morning off.

He'd have preferred Captain's for the big moment, but since she'd just had lunch there, the elegant, but-too-romantic-for-his-taste Italian restaurant would have to do.

Cucina's was looking pretty damned great to him by the time Priscilla's car pulled up in the drive in front of Jax's mansion. He was outside, ready to help her unload, before she was even out of her vehicle. Not at all fond of how off his game he was. Watching the clock? The window? Worrying?

Jax just wasn't *that* guy.

Or hadn't been until the first time he'd held his newborn son in his arms.

He managed to hold any, "is everything okay," "what took so long?" or, God forbid, "where've you been?" type catastrophes from his tongue, coming out with instead, "You've got your pick of garage stall spaces." As though a place to park her car was a major benefit to the potentially life-long favor she was doing for him.

From there, he grabbed her trunk and disappeared inside his place before he could further blunder and find it even more difficult to recognize himself.

Or give her second thoughts before they made it to the courthouse.

Priscilla didn't give indication of noticing anything off about him—not that she would, it wasn't like she knew him all that well. But then, Liam woke as she was heading up the stairs and Jax rated zero next to his son for the unique woman's attention.

A fact for which he was grateful. Immensely. For the most part.

It wasn't until she'd changed and they were in his Jaguar—a vehicle he didn't drive much as the truck was much more practical for his everyday use—on their way to Cucina's, at the Emerald Ridge Hotel, that he was finally alone with her.

"You didn't have to do this," she said, spreading a hand between the two of them. "I'd have been just fine eating something light at home."

Right. But then, she didn't know he'd been shopping. And to that point, he said, "If we want everyone to believe that we've been having a secret relationship that we're now bringing out into the open, then we need to actually be in the open," he told her. A build-up to the whole ring thing that was the main course on his menu for the evening.

He'd been debating with himself ever since making the purchase whether or not to give her a heads-up, or just play out the moment for real. If her surprise and delight in the beautiful piece of jewelry were genuine, it would be that much more convincing, and therefore, make it back to the Noveltys in a way that put their minds at ease. And eradicate any doubts they might still be harboring.

On the other hand...if she just looked shocked or appalled and tried to reject the grand gesture as not necessary given their circumstances, then he could be jeopardizing the publicly witnessed reassurance he was after.

Turned out, he didn't get the chance to make a decision one way or the other. Priscilla, in a sleek black, formfitting dress that fell a couple of inches above her knees, and matching high-heeled sandals with silver jewels across the straps, distracted his thoughts altogether.

"I told my uncle and brothers about us today," she said, her tone...even. Giving him nothing.

Glancing at her as he pulled to a stop at a light, he gained no more than that from her expression. "How'd it go?" he asked, getting himself worked up again.

The whole dad thing, knowing what was at stake—he wasn't handling it as well as he'd have expected. Or liked.

Ever since his ex-in-laws and then the petite, hazel-eyed woman had appeared in his path at the park on Monday, he'd been scrambling for his usual sense of confidence.

Tossing a strand of long blond hair over a partially bare shoulder, Priscilla said, "About as you'd expect."

He hoped to God not. His expectations were running along the lines of total train wreck at the moment. Glancing at her, he gave her a raised eyebrow. And nothing else.

"They were...concerned. Stating the short time that we could possibly have been dating—given that we've both only been back in Emerald Ridge for a month—they pretty much collectively suggested that we wait a bit. You know, the whole, why rush into marriage argument."

"Did you tell them why?" he asked. They were her family after all. If she'd felt as though she had to come clean, he wouldn't blame her.

She'd still shown up at his home, personal belongings in tow.

"I said, when you know, you know," she said simply. Without even a twitch of a finger. "And I know that marrying you is the right thing."

Her confidence was impressive.

And reassuring. "You really think that?" Lines between reality and their subterfuge were blurring.

She nodded, and when he pulled into the valet parking lane at the hotel and put the Jag in park, she asked, "Don't you?"

Jax was shocked to find that, with her sitting there— her fingers still on the handle that would open her door, while she sought his gaze—his own truth was right there, too.

He might not be able to answer the same to a vow involving loving and cherishing, but in the moment at hand, he could land the pitch with complete honesty.

"I do."

Chapter Five

As much as Priscilla had wanted to spend the evening at the Wellington Ranch to be with Liam, she found herself thoroughly enjoying the time out with Jax. Even knowing that he was putting on an act for all of the unknowing spectators around them, she was captivated by his attentiveness.

To the point that she worried how much of a goner she'd be if he ever turned on that charm at home. In the pursuit of a more personal, much more intimate, date. She knew the sex would be great. Just her body's unheard-of reaction to the man over the past few days was testament to that.

But what about her heart? She'd never been with a man who was able to arouse such intense physical awareness within her. So how did she know that other parts of her wouldn't be equally as captivated?

How could she be sure she wasn't already starting to feel more than empathy for him? It wasn't like she'd recognize the signs.

Sipping from the glass of champagne he'd ordered— a bottle to share between the two of them—she caught a glimpse of…appreciation in Jax's gaze as he looked back at her, and her crotch flooded with want. Just from the look.

One that was clearly only there for show.

From a man who had no ability or desire to ever fall in love.

She had to nip it all in the bud before she ruined things. Intense emotion, even sexually based, was a river filled with murky water. Every time one lifted a foot to take a step, she'd never know what she might be putting it back down upon. Safe ground? Or a sinkhole?

Just the not knowing part would lead to tension. Which changed one's perspective. Could shove a good mood into a bad one. Make a person snippy. Which led to hurt feelings. And even murkier waters. It was a vicious cycle.

No way could she risk falling into that river. The wayward emotion would ruin absolutely everything.

Not just for her, but for Liam and Jax, too.

Their marriage would be a disaster. They'd end up divorced. And…

Clearly there was only one option.

Definitely no sex between them. *Ever.*

Almost as though fate was laughing at her, Jax took a hold of her hand just as she'd solidified the choice with a gallon of resolve. She watched, mouth open, as he slid down to one knee directly in front of her, and, with his other hand, pulled a small box out of his pocket.

She was in the middle of a bizarre dream. One that in real life would be a nightmare. Staring, knowing that it wasn't real, but unable to stop what would come next.

Or prevent what it would do to her.

With a flip of his thumb, Jax opened the box, and moving it closer to her said, "Priscilla Fortune, would you do me the honor of becoming my wife?"

She tried to answer. To play the game. Couldn't speak. Not a word. She just stared. Growing more increasingly aware of the ramifications that were closing in on her. The people watching from other tables. A waiter with a full tray balanced on one hand at his shoulder, stopping just behind Jax.

Her heart pounding like the proposal was for real. Not just for show.

Staring at the ring, she felt tears prick the backs of her eyes. Had to blink before anyone noticed. To stop her lips from trembling.

"I promise to be faithful to you and our life together," Jax said then, his tone so oddly soft she had to look up from the ring to him. "To be present and honest. To keep your needs in the mix at all times. And to uphold my responsibilities to you, to the marriage and to our son."

Tears flooded her eyes then and scared her to death. She didn't understand them. Or the intensity flowing through her veins. But she understood his words.

And knew that he was speaking the truth.

Which freed her own. "Yes, Jax, I'll marry you…" she said, somewhat shakily due to the overwhelming emotion coursing through her—clearly a result of the act they were putting on—but got no further as the entire room burst into applause and cheers around them.

She heard the cacophony like thunder in a storm as Jax slid the ring on her finger, and, still holding her hand, stood, pulling her up with him.

He slid an arm around her back and turned them to face the room, with a small bow. It was all very theatrical, in a way, but seemed genuine, too. Appropriate to the moment.

Her racing heart, the excitement coursing through her, were not.

The smile on her face was so big it hurt, so she gave herself a pat on the back for being a much better actor than she'd thought. Until realization hit her smack in the face.

The proposal might have been planned to convince others that she and Jax were in love, but the question he had asked, the promises he'd made—and her response to him—they *were* all real.

The marriage she'd just agreed to, publicly, was going to happen. And be legally binding.

Waiting for another wave of panic, for the nightmarish cloud to overtake her, Priscilla glanced up at Jax and felt…peace…instead.

Before she could process even that, a strange sense of happiness washed over her, filling her heart. Her own brand of excitement, not society's definition of what should make her feel that way. And warmth didn't just fade away. It coated her. Seemed to fit.

Right up until Jax lowered his head to place his lips on her open mouth.

Then the flood pooled lower.

And dread came rushing back.

Jax didn't let himself think about the personal ramifications of the choice he was making. Men went into battle every day to make life better for their children, their loved ones, their communities and countries. If he looked back, he stood to get shot in the face.

He had to keep his mind on the goal. Every day had to be about cultivating a life that would be healthy and happy for Liam. Which meant the life had to be that way for Priscilla Fortune, too. Whatever it took to keep her happy, he'd signed on to provide.

It was really that simple for him.

As long as he didn't get dragged down by overthinking, second-guessing, or an insidious fear of failing.

Proposing had turned out to be kind of fun. The genuine surprise on Priscilla's face had captivated him, to the point of forgetting the other diners around them, or the fact that he'd planned them as witnesses. The whole promise thing had just come to him.

And the kiss…impromptu as it had been, might have been preordained. If one actually believed in such things.

One kiss and his misgivings about the road upon which he'd embarked had just faded away. Not because it was the hottest kiss he'd ever had. Not even close.

But it had been the most *honest*. An expression of gratitude, a promise to be trustworthy, with something more tantalizing behind the scenes. Neither he nor Priscilla had any way of knowing what the future would hold for them, but they could count on each to head toward it together.

Which was more than he'd ever had as an adult.

More than he'd ever expected to have.

Or that he thought he wanted to have. And yet…he *did* want it.

And not just for Liam.

The idea of a real home, with him running the ranch upon which he'd grown up…who'd have thought there'd be such power in the thought of such a thing? Certainly not him.

And doing it with a woman who was not only okay that he didn't do the whole fall in love thing—who wouldn't have expectations of him that would set them both up for failure—was almost too good to be true.

Yet, true it was.

The downfall, a life of celibacy, was a cross he was willing to bear—and a seemingly small price to pay—for the great bounty he'd been given. Some cold showers, or not so cold ones, alone in his room, would take care of his physical hungers well enough.

Not that he'd ever had to test that theory for more than a month or two. From the time he'd hit puberty women much older than himself had been making themselves available to him. He hadn't availed himself until he'd been old enough to do them justice, but he'd never had to go looking when he was ready. He also hadn't kidded himself that it was him, the person, they wanted. More like the Wellington looks and money that they were after.

A summation his father hadn't seemed to be able to make.

Unless, had the elder Wellington known that money was all that Courtney had been after? Had he brought the woman into their family knowing that?

Jax wasn't sure which scenario was preferable. That his father had been hoodwinked—and hurt. Or that he hadn't been and had exposed his kids, *their heritage*, to a crook just for the satisfaction of having a young, beautiful wife.

Looking at the woman riding beside him in his expensive vehicle on the way back to the Wellington Ranch— where they'd both be living in a home they'd be sharing for the foreseeable future—Jax caught her looking down at the ring he'd placed on her finger just before their dinner had arrived.

She hadn't eaten much.

But then, neither had he. They'd spent too much time talking to those who'd stopped by their table, one party at a time, to wish them congratulations.

Until he'd suggested they take doggy bags home, at which point she'd flashed him a grateful smile. The first time she'd looked him in the eye since he'd kissed her.

He never should have done that. And would have told her so if he'd had any explanation for his behavior.

"If you'd like something else, we can exchange it," he said, glancing down at the ring. Not sure what he thought of himself, feeling all proud to have been the one to put such an exquisite piece of jewelry on that particular finger.

It was like he was taking the whole thing for real. Which it was. Just not for the expected and assumed reasons.

"No." The one word didn't give him much, and Jax started to get concerned again. Had the whole public arena thing been too much? Was she having major regrets? Getting ready to tell him she'd changed her mind?

"You sure? Because…"

"I'm sure, Jax," she said, her tone firm enough to convince him. He could feel her gaze on him, see it peripherally, but used his need to keep the car on the road as an excuse not to glance over. He wasn't sure he wanted to find out what she might be telling him.

"I love the ring," she reiterated. "I was about ready to ask if you'd talked to Zara about it. She's the only one I've ever had a conversation with about wedding rings."

"I haven't spoken to your sister since she was about fifteen," he said. "She had a thing for a friend of mine. I told her not to trust him, and she never spoke to me again."

"Did she ever go out with the guy?"

"Not that I know of. It was his last summer in town. And just to be clear, it's not like she ever spoke to me before that, either." He'd been too busy fending off the seventeen- and eighteen-year-old socialites to be accessible to the younger girls. Not that he'd minded at the time.

He'd learned a lot since then.

"You talked to Zara about the kind of engagement ring you wanted?" This from a woman who'd said she didn't want any part of falling in love and getting married?

Priscilla's chuckle gave him a tug in the fly area. "Calm down, Jax," she said. "It was a couple of years ago, and in the years since you've known her, my perennially single older sister has become quite the matchmaker. She was trying to get me to imagine the perfect ring, as though that would somehow translate to me finding the man who'd magically show up and propose. Once I got her drift, I quit the game. Seriously…as though a ring would be all it would take for a man to sweep me off my feet. Anyway, I was thinking that, after my conversation with my male family members today, who would have immediately passed on the news to the rest, maybe she'd called you…"

He wasn't sure that's what she'd been thinking. At least not until he'd asked if she liked the ring. It bothered him how much he wanted to know what she *had* been thinking.

So he asked, "You having second thoughts about us?" The couple of seconds of silence that followed had him forging ahead, feeling like one of his bulls in the kitchen, as he asked, "It was a lot back there. I hadn't foreseen how it would all play out, and I apologize if it was too overwhelming."

Her silence stretched longer. Jax was excruciatingly

aware that she hadn't answered his initial query. Was she changing her mind?

It would pretty much make him the laughingstock of their elite community in the small town where his son would be raised, but since, with Courtney, that ship had already sailed, Jax didn't give a full whit on that one.

He did, however, struggle to breathe freely as he thought about the possible ramifications for Liam once the Noveltys got word. Making his plan feel like the biggest backfire of all time.

But the letdown was more than that. Something he couldn't explain. Like he was losing her friendship, like it *mattered*, when it wasn't anything he'd ever had.

"I'm not having second thoughts about us." The words came softly through the darkness, and had the effect of a sudden burst of sunshine on him. Until his brain acknowledged the hesitancy in the statement. That, and the length of time it had taken her to come out with the response, left those second thoughts still on the table.

"But?" he asked, when she seemed content to leave her statement as is.

"I'm not having second thoughts," she repeated, with much more oomph behind the words. Had she issued them that way a moment before he'd have pulled into his driveway and maneuvered into the garage with ease.

As it was, he parked, but then turned to look at her. "Tell me," he demanded. And when she shook her head and reached for her door handle, he knew he couldn't let it go.

Reaching out to touch her shoulder, he said in a softer tone, "Please?" And saw the lines creasing her forehead by the garage light shining down on them through the windshield.

"I'm not having second thoughts, Jax. I know this is the right decision for me."

"And yet, still, I hear a but there." He wasn't imagining things. Those hazel eyes currently had shadows in them.

"There is no but."

Okay. Fine. "Then what is there? Because you're different. And while I'm no expert on relationships, one thing I do know is that this isn't going to work if we aren't honest with each other. If we can't trust each other."

Her gaze cleared some then, as she met his gaze. And she nodded. "Fine," she told him. "But...you aren't going to like it."

He'd already figured that much out for himself. Just had to know how *much* he wasn't going to like it. And what he could do to make it better.

He waited.

"It's us," she confessed.

Jax sat back. Nonplussed. Thinking he'd misheard her. "Us?" he asked.

She was changing her mind? Backing out.

"I told you you weren't going to like it," Priscilla said then, reaching for her door handle again. "You ready to go in?"

Seriously? After that? "No." The word came out before he'd made the final decision to issue it, but he wasn't sorry. "What about us?"

"I'm feeling more like a friend then a business associate."

A where are we headed conversation? Oh. God.

He should have taken the out she'd offered. That one word, *no*, and suddenly he was wading in muck.

Figuring he was dealing with the proverbial sticky bandage that just had to come off fast, he said, "Business associates can be friends," he told her.

Her gaze narrowed on him. "They say not to mix business with pleasure."

He nodded. "They'd probably say not to get married for the reasons we're doing so, too. In our case, I'd say friendship bodes well for the success of the venture. Plus, it sets a good example for Liam, to watch the friendship between his parents."

He was spitballing. And seeing validity in the stuff he was spewing without thought, too. Her gaze was locked on his. As though afraid to completely trust what she was hearing. Which immediately prompted him to add,

"I'm finding myself valuing your friendship, too."

There. Good. He'd done it. Been honest. And even with his heart a little bit out there, was still in one piece.

"Well, thank goodness!" Priscilla was suddenly all smiles. The woman he'd seen in the park on Monday when they'd just been chatting. The one who'd held out her hand to him later as a seal of agreement. "It's good to know we're on the same page," he told Priscilla, and followed the words with a genuinely happy smile as he said, "We should go in. Liam's going to be up soon, and ready to eat." And Jax would spend the night hauling his ass out of bed every two hours to make sure his son got the nourishment his growing body craved.

Same as every other night since he'd been back in Emerald Ridge.

With one exception. Starting that night, he and Liam would no longer be alone in their home.

Priscilla Fortune would be there with them.

For better or worse.

Until death did them part.

The vow was Jax's prayer as he followed the beautiful Fortune heir into their home.

He just wasn't sure the prayer was heard.

Or that he was ready and worthy to have it be so.

Chapter Six

After the unexpected evening out, and the way her body had responded to Jax's completely platonic kiss—one that she'd known was only a show put on for those who'd report back to his ex-in-laws—Priscilla gave in when Jax insisted that since she was just getting settled in, he'd cover all Liam duties for that first night. She didn't even pretend to argue. Just nodded and wished him good night, leaving him to see Sasha out and escort the housekeeper to her little cottage on the property for the night.

Sasha, the Wellington Ranch full-time housekeeper/babysitter—who, Priscilla had heard, had been with the family since before Jax was born, but had quit after Annelise moved out to be with Drake and Courtney had been the only Wellington left on the property.

Priscilla remembered hearing in all the talk about Courtney Wellington's arrest and subsequent imprisonment that Annelise had been responsible for bringing the housekeeper home as a surprise for Jax, to not only help keep the house in tip-top shape but also to assist in caring for Liam when the nanny she'd also hired couldn't be there.

She hoped Jax's sister would be at least open to welcoming Priscilla into their small family unit. And didn't like the idea that with his sister on a multicountry bonding trip with her new fiancé and his long-lost twin, Jax had no way of letting Annelise know of his marriage plans.

The woman was going to arrive home with a sister-in-law in residence whom she'd only known peripherally more than a decade before. The shock alone could have a negative impact. Add in the fact that Jax and Priscilla had only "dated" for a month before becoming engaged, and Priscilla could be facing a double whammy on that front.

Nothing she couldn't handle. Just something to worry about during her trip into town the next morning during Sasha's time with Liam. Anything to keep her mind off the night she'd just spent, listening to Jax on the other side of her bedroom wall, crooning to his son as he changed and fed him.

Her heart had burst open during those hours, oozing out all over her room, lining the air with a sense of want that she feared would be forever there. Every single time she stepped in Jax's home. And most particularly in her room at night.

She wanted the man. Wanted his arms around her.

And so much more. She wanted their marriage to be based on their feelings for each other, not just mutual needs. Wanted to know that he cared about her.

Which was so ludicrous she could hardly bear to sit with herself in the car as she sped toward a haven she'd never visited before. The Emerald Ridge Hot Spring, part of a natural preserve, was not only known for its relaxation and healing properties, but to help people with troubling decisions as well.

Not one to put a lot of stock in hot water being able to

cure the world, Priscilla was desperate just to rediscover her ability to relax. A lack of which was brand-new to her.

Once she could get into her quiet mode, her choices would line up in rows as they always did. And good decisions would follow. Except that they didn't. In her one-piece black swimsuit, she'd found a quiet, secluded spot along the natural rock wall, had slid down into the healing warmth and thought about the journal she'd found the day before.

The dream she'd had for her future. And tried to figure out when she'd let it go. Couldn't. Then wondered why it mattered.

Closing her eyes, she allowed herself to savor the physical comfort of the hot spring. Tried to breathe in peace. But took in energy instead. A need to get going. Doing. To pick up the few things she needed in town and get back to the Wellington Ranch.

Her new home.

So why wasn't she there? Staking her claim?

Jax's kiss. She'd never known anything like her response to it. Wanted it to have been because of the fairy tale moment he'd created, but knew that it was not. His lips…they were soft where they needed to be, and yet relayed a sense of strength, of purposeful temptation to a journey he could take her on, of an ability to pleasure that seemed more natural than the water she was soaking in.

But that wasn't all of it. His conversation at dinner, his awareness of her changing moods, were both new. It was like the man was the vision of her childish dream for her future life.

But she knew better than anyone that life didn't work that way. With a disruptive splash, Priscilla stood, got herself dried and decently covered, then, with her towel and wet suit in hand, she strode with purpose back along the preserve's paths to her car.

She'd found no magic eraser for the feelings that had erupted all over her the night before, but she'd discovered that she didn't need one. She simply had to keep her head out of the clouds, and remain firmly in a present that had more to offer her than she'd had in a long while.

By the time she'd acquired the couple of things she'd gone into town to get, and had stopped for a chai latte for the drive back, she was happy again. Herself. Aware, confident, in control of her destiny and pleased with where it was leading her. Until she caught a glimpse of the elevator she'd taken with Jax the night before and was swamped with emotion again.

Not all bad. But not boding well, either.

Why she'd come into the Emerald Ridge Café— located in the Emerald Ridge Hotel lobby—for the tea, she had no idea. It was like she had some bone to pick with herself. Egging herself on until…what?

The sight of a familiar Stetson saved Priscilla from the nowhere conversation going on in her head. "Harris!"

She called out her brother's name as she approached his table. With too much enthusiasm she was sure, on both counts. The calling and the approach. But it was shutting up her internal voices.

An international businessman and very confirmed bachelor, Harris was always fun to talk to. More, he had such interesting things to say that she was never bored with him. Nor did her mind wander off on its own.

Of course, she'd failed to take into account the fact that her older brother by four years was going to want to question her more about her shocking announcement the day before.

Except that…he didn't. He just stood as she approached, looked her in the eye for an uncomfortably long time, and then, waiting for her to take her seat, stood with a hand on his own chair. The one with his Stetson hanging from it.

"That's some ring," he told her, eyeing the new jewelry on her left hand.

She glanced down and smiled. *Hugely.* She couldn't help herself. The sight of the ring brought back instant visions of the romantic fantasy Jax had created the night before. For a second or two, she'd been the princess in the magical fairy tale. Loved and adored wholly and completely.

For that brief moment, she'd come first in someone else's life.

The thought stopped her cold.

Come first? What was that?

And yet, watching as her brother left her to head to the counter to place her order, everyone in the family knew that chai latte was it, every time… Priscilla couldn't shake the errant thought.

Checked it. When *had* she come first? When did anyone come first in anyone else's life?

When they were born. In moments when they had their parents' full attention…

She'd been a kid when her parents had died. The youngest kid. And had become part of the Fortune crowd after that…

Harris pulled her attention back to reality as he approached with her tea, in the to-go cup she always preferred.

Because he knew her that well. All of her siblings did. Just as she knew them. She didn't have to come first. She was part of a foursome that would always be there. No matter what.

Except that... Roth was with Antonia now, and she and her little girl would be coming first in his life. Just as Liam had changed Jax's priorities. Hell, Jax, the confirmed bachelor, was actually getting married in spite of his natural abhorrence of the institution—just for Liam.

Her brother took his seat, his blond hair a little long and nonconformist—as normal to her as her penchant for chai.

"I have to say, there's definitely something different about you," he said, eyebrows raised as he looked at her.

Afraid of what he'd see, she remembered the night before, the swoonworthy proposal, and smiled. "I think I am different," she told him. "Just like Roth is," she added, mostly because their eldest brother had just been on the tip of her tongue. Shrugging, she added, "It happens..."

And was running out of platitudes. If Harris dug deeper...what would he find?

It wasn't the day for a family inquisition. She was out of sorts. Wasn't herself.

She was saved from her self-induced panic as Harris's attention was suddenly focused behind Priscilla and a female voice said, "Oh, I'm so glad I saw you two!"

Priscilla didn't know the voice, but she recognized the stylishly dressed elderly woman who stopped at their table. She just couldn't remember from where.

"I'm Vera Duff," the woman said, looking between the two of them.

Harris smiled. "You own Emerald Ridge Camera and Photo," he said. And Priscilla had a vague memory about some patent her brother had once pursued that had something to do with film. Or a camera lens. Or something to that effect. Harris had been chasing investments ever since she could remember. And had become a powerful force in the business world in his own right because of it.

"That's right," Vera said, smiling at them both, "and I've been meaning to get in touch with you all. I'm selling my shop, and things are getting moved around and I came across a big pack of negatives that ended up wedged behind a cabinet I just sold. Turns out the negatives are all your baby and childhood photos." As Priscilla's mouth fell open, the woman just kept right on talking, as though she hadn't just landed a priceless bombshell on her two recipients. "I can't recall if Marlene had them developed or not, but, knowing your mother, she probably did. You all probably have all the photos, but I wanted to offer you the negatives before I just throw them away…"

"We'll take them," Harris said quickly.

And Priscilla added, "I'll come get them right now."

"Oh, I'm sorry, dear, I'm on my way out of town for the day. But I'll be in the shop in the morning if you'd like to get them then."

Nodding so hard her hair fell over her shoulders, Priscilla said, "I'll be there." Agreeing to the 9:00 a.m. time before she realized that she'd have Liam with her then.

Because she wasn't just a single, carefree woman with volunteer time on her hands anymore. Or much free time, either.

She'd agreed to be a mother to a three-month-old baby.

And while she should be feeling daunted by that fact, Priscilla just wasn't.

But she had another errand to take care of before she went back to the ranch.

She had to buy an infant car seat with the highest safety rating.

And learn how to navigate it.

As Jax came in from a hard day of repairing sabotaged fencing, he felt more energetic than he had since his return to Emerald Ridge. Just three days had passed since his meeting in the park with Christa's parents.

Monday to Thursday.

A passing from one lifetime to the next.

It had been happening a lot to him lately. His life changing on a dime. He'd gone from a carefree—albeit investor in earth friendly projects—bachelor breaking up with a casual fling to being a father in the space of one sentence. Christa's *I'm pregnant.*

From a married father to a widowed single dad with another phone call. *Mr. Wellington? We regret to inform you...*

And a stop at a jeweler's and a simple, *will you do me the honor*, had completely changed his life again.

Good news was, this time there'd been no shock. No grief. No heart sinking.

No dread.

Just trepidation. Doubts. Resolutions. And a whole lot of gratitude.

Taking the double wide boards on the grand staircase two at a time, Jax went straight for the nursery. Sasha had only been on duty until noon that day. Priscilla, on her first day of surrogate motherhood, was likely in need of a break.

And perhaps Jax was in need of reaffirmation that the newest life he was embarking on was actually going to be a positive change for all three of them.

He also wanted to inspect the work he'd had done. The contractor had sent photos throughout the day and his housekeeper had texted when the cleaning crew was through. He hadn't heard from Priscilla though.

His stopping point. How did he know…

What? That everything was fine? He hadn't texted her, either.

Rounding the corner quietly, figuring Liam for another half hour's sleep at a minimum, Jax had a grin on his face as he first entered the room.

An expression that slowly diminished as he saw the empty crib. And rocking chair.

He glanced at the new door that had been constructed between the nursery and Priscilla's suite—making the nursery a walk-through from hers to his—and then pulled out his phone.

He texted. Didn't want a ring to wake the baby.

And heard back immediately. Priscilla and Liam were outside in the garden by the pool, getting some fresh air.

A normal activity for a mother and her child. A shock to his system. Texting back that he was going to take a quick shower, Jax didn't wait to hear Priscilla's response before he stripped down and stepped under the spray.

In the month since he'd been a single father no one had taken his son out of the nursery without Jax being privy to the information. He was the boss. The father. The sole decision-maker.

And…now he wasn't. And really hadn't been. Liam was so young, and sleeping so much of the time still, that

Liam's nanny hadn't had opportunity for outings yet. But neither had the older woman literally sat in Liam's nursery all day. She'd brought him down to other parts of the house. Had put him in his swing in the garden room as well as the playpen in the living room. She'd texted photos, too. Every time.

Priscilla hadn't.

Nor had he asked her to. Or in any way indicated that she should. In fairness to…he didn't know who…he hadn't even thought about any of it.

He'd bought a ring. Proposed. Talked about friendship. And ordered a door. But the logistics of him and Priscilla Fortune sharing a home, a life, a baby, hadn't once been discussed.

What kind of father did that make him?

More, what kind of *engaged* man?

Figuring he'd get his dinner out of the way so he could take responsibility for Liam for the night as soon as Priscilla brought him in, Jax dressed in jeans and a black T-shirt and flip-flops and made his way to the immense kitchen, remembering a time when his mother and Sasha had been getting ready for some big fancy party and he'd decided that was the moment to practice floor surfing in his socks. With the kitchen floor being the largest space in which to master his skill.

He'd flown right into a young woman carrying a tray of little bowls filled with green Jell-O, and all three of them had ended up in a pile of goo on the tile.

He couldn't remember any more than that. Didn't recall being punished, or even yelled at, but it had probably happened. Mostly what he remembered was that he was done floor surfing anywhere but the upstairs hallway.

Which hadn't been nearly as much fun, all closed in by walls as it had been. How did you swerve and ride waves if you could only go straight?

Instead of the slow cooked barbecued beef and layered salad being plated for him as they'd been every night since he'd returned to the ranch a month ago, both were still in serving dishes. In portions large enough to feed an entire family.

Pulling out the beef, as it needed to reheat, he laid it on the massive prep counter in the middle of the room and was heading for a plate when he heard sounds in the hall. A voice.

Softly singing? Frozen with his hand in midair, he listened. Recognized the tune, some nursery rhyme thing from his childhood. Couldn't remember the words. But it wouldn't have mattered. They weren't the same.

"Here we go now, here we go now, little Liam, little Liam..." with an emphasis on the last part of his son's name to fit the tune.

In a voice that was...beautiful. Not just the ability to carry the tune, but the tonal quality...

Lost in enjoying the moment, Jax almost dropped the plate he'd secured when Liam's stroller pushed through the kitchen door, followed right behind by petite, blonde and beautiful, Priscilla Fortune.

His gaze sought hers, then immediately shied away, landing on her hands pushing his son—which were fully engrossed by the huge sparkling diamond Jax had put there.

She stopped when she saw him. "I thought you were in the shower," she said, in a tone completely different from the playful song she'd been singing to his much younger counterpart.

"I figured I'd get my meal out of the way so I can take over there." He nodded toward his son.

"Oh." She glanced away from Jax. Pointedly. Her gaze glued on the stroller. "I...apologize. I told Sasha not to bother making up a plate, that we'd eat together..." She turned then, with the stroller halfway through the door, and said, "I'll just take him upstairs and get him changed and fed so he'll be ready for you."

Several things hit Jax at once. Preventing him from stopping her exit.

He'd hurt her feelings. Which wasn't supposed to happen.

Liam was up way earlier than he'd thought. Or perhaps had slept much later at some point during the day, putting him off his schedule.

And Jax was no longer hungry.

Chapter Seven

She felt like a fool. All afternoon those negatives she'd be getting in the morning from the photo shop had been on Priscilla's mind. Coming and going in the forefront, but always there. She'd been planning to tell Jax about them over dinner.

Just to be able to talk it over with someone they didn't involve.

And…she trusted him with her private stuff. Something that Priscilla almost never did.

Both thoughts brought her up short as she pulled a contented Liam out of his stroller and carried him up the grand staircase to the nursery.

They'd had to move downstairs the second the remodeling crew had hit, which had been about ten minutes after Priscilla had gotten home.

Of course she trusted Jax. She wouldn't be marrying him otherwise. Wouldn't have moved into his home overnight.

But on what grounds? And why not every other nice person she met? Or one with major needs that she could help fill?

Her entire adult life consisted of the latter. Her spending her days satisfying the needs of others. It made her feel good. Gave purpose to her life.

But Jax had been different from the first moment she'd seen him again that summer. With his baby in tow... needing her help adopting a couple of dogs...his seeming vulnerability when she knew him to be a man who was anything but.

"Hey." She jumped when she heard his voice behind her. Thankfully, she'd just laid Liam on the changing table. And stepped back immediately, keeping a hand on the baby's feet as she waited for Jax to take his rightful place in front of his son. He hadn't seen him all day.

Priscilla had had several wonderful hours with the precious little one.

As she moved, he quickly stepped up. His hands automatically tending to the changing detail, and Priscilla was impressed with, and admittedly a tad bit jealous of, his supreme competence. She'd already learned that Liam's patience was usually divvied up in portions of seconds, not minutes.

And had earned herself some angry screams that afternoon.

"Listen," he said, one diaper off, the other sliding under as a wipe expertly appeared. "I screwed up the whole dinner thing. I'm sorry. I would appreciate a dinner companion, if the offer is still open. I'm just...in a routine, and haven't wrapped my mind around how all this is going to work. You know, the changes that will be happening." He had the diaper on, the sleeper snapped and Liam in his arms as he turned around—having been talking the entire time. "Maybe we can discuss it all over dinner? Which I can be ready for in say, half an hour?"

He'd already pulled a bottle of premade formula out of the small refrigerator in the nursery and had it in the warmer.

Priscilla should have felt dismissed. Ordered to go make dinner. But didn't. At all. Smiling at Jax—who was calmly taking on daddy duties after being out in the field all day, and dealing with a new woman in his mix, too— she grew more in like with him.

You could date a man for six months and not see as much of real person as she'd just witnessed in five minutes with Jax Wellington.

"I'll have dinner waiting," she told him, and skedaddled before she embarrassed herself with some kind of praise comment.

One that would put her in the murky waters she knew she'd drown in.

She'd had her hot water fix for the day.

And needed to keep her head way above the waves so she didn't screw up what might very well turn out to be the best thing that had ever happened to her.

Baby monitor receiver in hand, Jax came to the dinner table with a full agenda. The way he avoided future missteps with the woman who was saving his life was to have clear expectations on both sides. Meaning, he had to be as clear as she was as to what she expected of him.

She'd already met the only expectation he could have of her. Agreeing to marry him. The rest… Liam's care… was a whole second piece of cake as far as he was concerned. He could have continued on as he was—paying Bonita, the nanny Annelise had hired, for daytime care while he took nights.

And Priscilla came and went as she pleased.

The marriage was the one thing he couldn't handle on his own. And the only thing that was going to keep the Noveltys from trying to rip his son from his heritage, his birthright and Jax's care.

And for that legal joining he'd pay by meeting every expectation Priscilla Fortune had of him. Come hell or high water.

She was in the kitchen when he came down, her petite body in the black T-shirt dress seeming to fill the massive space as she leaned casually against a side counter, her phone screen held up to her face. Her hair, which had been in a ponytail earlier, was loose and flowing around her shoulders. For a second Jax just stood there in the far doorway leading in from the dining room, watching her.

Almost memorizing the moment. For what purpose he didn't understand. He just stood there, transfixed, until she moved, and he feared being discovered. "He fell right to sleep," he said then, galvanized into action. Which meant continuing on into the kitchen. "I'm early. You want some help getting things on?"

She was a Fortune. Had grown up with even more of a household staff than he had. She wasn't there to wait on him.

"All set," she told him, setting her phone on the counter to slide her hand into a thermal glove and pull plates out of the kitchen's newest addition. An air fryer. He'd acquainted himself with the thing half a dozen times in the month he'd been back.

Mostly just to make toast at two in the morning. With peanut butter slathered on it. Helped keep him awake while his son ate.

Who needed a fryer thing to make toast?

He'd discovered—after a night of hunting for the toaster to no avail, only to have Sasha educate him the next morning—that the new appliance was an all in one.

Priscilla seemed to already be fully cognizant of the oven's multiple capabilities, and it made him wonder... "When you're here, in your place on the estate for the summer, do you have staff?"

He'd hire them. Give Sasha extra help and...

"No," she said, shaking her head. "The housekeeping staff at the main house keeps all four of the cottages clean, anyway. And we all only intended to be here for a few days—a week at the most."

"So you do your own cooking?"

With a mitt on each hand, she carried two plates from the warmer to the dining room, saying, "Sometimes. Mostly I eat out. Or up at the main house with everyone else."

"But you *can* cook."

"Yep."

He turned, his gaze following her as she passed him to head back into the kitchen, where she pulled out two bowls from the refrigerator, and went by him a third time as she carried those in.

"There's a bottle of Mendoza wine there if you want to uncork and pour," she murmured. "I'm assuming Sasha left it because she knows your preference."

He had a glass at dinner every night. But... "We can skip it. Or choose something else if you'd like."

With a grin, she pulled out a chair and sat. The one perpendicular to the end seating he'd been using since his return. "I've been looking forward to a glass of that since Sasha showed it to me this afternoon."

Uncorking the wine, Jax grabbed two glasses from the rack inside a glass-fronted cupboard, and joined her. "Did she show you the rest of the collection?"

"What's left of it you mean? She said that Courtney did a number on that, too. Claiming that some of the bottles had been tainted or something?"

He shook his head. Tried to keep himself away from the gossip. It was in the court's hand, and as he'd been absent during Courtney's entire reign of terror, they needed nothing from him. "Other than the cleanup the ranch required by her sabotage, I'm steering clear of anything the woman said, did or touched," he bit out.

And then, glancing at Priscilla in a new light, said, "But your brother's a vintner, right? Quite an exclusive one, from what I've heard."

"My oldest brother, Roth, yes," she told him, smiling.

"You ever have anything to do with his business?"

"Other than playing hostess at various functions, no. But I've learned enough about wine to open a winery if I ever chose to do so." She was smiling, as she held up the glass he'd just filled and handed to her, and he held up his own as well.

Toasting her silently, he sipped. Set his glass down then asked, "So you have any interest in restocking our supply here?"

With a grin hinting at her lips, she frowned. "Depends on how much I have at my disposal to spend and how much say I have in the product choices."

His chuckle surprised him. Just bubbling up naturally.

He couldn't remember the last time that had happened. If ever. "Carte blanche."

"For which? The money or the choices?"

"Both."

Her face sobering, she shook her head. "You aren't paying for everything, Jax. Not if I'm an equal member of this odd little family we're creating. I'll concede to the Wellington Ranch upkeep being all you as it's Liam's inheritance, and I have my own seat on the board, so to speak, on both my family estate here, and in Dallas. However, living expenses, including luxuries and trips, and most particular Liam's needs and care, are handled together. Discussed, and paid for together." Holding out a hand, she said, "We can set up an investment account, both put the same amount of money in it, and live off of it. If we invest enough, and do it right, it will keep us throughout our lifetime. My brother Harris is a whiz at that, or we can have someone else handle the investments for us. Again, discuss and decide together. But bottom line is, we're a family or we're not. I'm either in, or I'm out."

Throat tight, Jax waited until he could swallow and then took a sip of wine. With every word she'd spoken, his muscles had tensed more and more. The sharing…they'd discuss. He'd buy her one hell of a lot of presents if he felt inclined to do so. But the demand… Priscilla's definition of family…took him back to being a kid in that very home. Hearing his mom talking about his dad to someone. He couldn't remember who. Wasn't even sure if he'd known. He just remembered the reverence in her voice as she'd described the relationship his dad had offered her. Expecting her to be in on every decision.

She'd said something about knowing that that's when she'd found her forever home.

Something he'd ceased believing in—or looking for—so long ago he couldn't remember ever having done so. But in that moment, remembering from the perspective of that little guy—he felt…happy…inside.

Standing, Jax left the table, the room, in a near sprint. In his office, he unlocked the bottom, fireproof file drawer of his desk, the one that held any important papers that weren't in a lockbox at the bank. Then he pulled out the folder of work he'd done with his lawyer the day before, and had finalized electronic payments with first thing that morning.

Back in the door of the dining room in just a few strides, his gaze shot immediately to Priscilla's empty chair and bare place setting, too. Glancing through the opposite door of the three entrance room, he saw her heading toward the grand staircase.

"Priscilla?" he called, hurrying behind her. "Wait up!"

Turning, she nearly glared at him. He missed the whole effect of the look, as his gaze landed on the plate, bowl, silverware, glass of wine and napkin balanced in her hands and arms.

"I don't…what's going on?" he asked, trying to catch up.

"I'm heading up to my room to finish dinner and think," she told him. "I just gave you an ultimatum, probably not the brightest idea without having considered what I'd do if you did what you just did and chose the *or else* part of it. For some reason, I'm not myself around you. Probably the whole major life change thing we're doing, but I'm feeling too emotional and need some time to my-self."

All Jax could say right then was, "Thank God you have a penchant for long explanations."

When her mouth dropped open, he reached for the ma-jority of her burden, sliding his folder between her elbow and her ribs as he did so, and, turning, headed back to the dining room.

Jax made a bit of a production of resetting her place— mostly to buy himself some time. Twice he'd seen her that evening. Twice he'd hurt her feelings. Priscilla Fortune most definitely was more prone to emotional upset than he'd ever be, but her honesty regarding the two of them, their relationship, was refreshing.

She was giving him a kindergarten class for one on dealing with feelings.

But…he was, so far, understanding the lessons, which gave him the ability to tend to situations before they esca-lated into something over which he had no control.

Taking her on, marrying her, he was facing one hell of a learning curve, but becoming a father had smacked him with the same type of challenge, and he'd been pass-ing that class. He could ace another.

Jax didn't look at Priscilla again until he'd taken his own seat. And had a healthy sip of wine warming his chest on the way to his stomach. She was standing by her chair, looking at the folder he'd given her.

Then dropped down to her seat.

Staring at him.

Priscilla really had just been going up to her room to regroup. She wasn't ready to pull the plug on the new future unfolding before her. And had pushed too hard. In hindsight, her first dinner with Jax should most definitely not have been ultimatum time.

Being the youngest of four powerful individuals who had enough money to move mountains, she'd had to learn early how to push or be pushed.

Or...push back when necessary.

Probably why she'd gotten into so many scraps as a kid and a young teen. She'd always taken on the fight, usually someone else's who was being pushed around.

But...just...wow. Never ever had she had such incredible results from her attempts to stand up for herself or others.

"When were you going to share this with me?" she asked quietly. Regarding the information in the folder— down to the right to adopt Liam, followed by her gaining full custody of the baby were anything to happen to Jax—she had no coherent thoughts forming.

He'd already put in legal motion bounty for her way beyond what she'd even thought to fight for.

"The day of the wedding," he told her. Then took a bite of barbecued meat as though anything about the moment was normal.

While she stared, he chewed. Swallowed. And then said, "It's not valid until after the ceremony. That's when it goes into effect." He nodded toward the folder as though he was merely sharing what was in it.

Which she was sure he was doing. But everything that was in it...

She had no idea what to say. And ended up with, "So, we agree. I'm in."

With an odd grin that sent a flash of desire through

her, he nodded. Waved a fork toward her food and said, "You might want to get on that. Sasha's beef is the best and it's getting cold."

She went for the wine first. Easiest to swallow. And would hopefully help her relax enough to do justice to the hard work the housekeeper had put in that day.

And after a couple of bites, and another sip or two of wine, she was able to form some coherent thoughts. "I bought a car seat today," she told him. Then with a second thought added, "And a houseful of other baby paraphernalia, too, for my cottage on the river. I figure I'll take Liam over there sometimes when you're working. My family and I are on a serious hunt for something my parents left us, and I still need to do my share to help out. Everything was delivered today, though I haven't been there to set it all up like I want it yet. But you're welcome to come out for lunch tomorrow and inspect if you'd like."

He nodded. Sipped. Nodded again. Drawing attention to the stiffness in his chin.

"What?" she asked him. And then thought of her ultimatum. "I should have talked to you, before outfitting my place for baby occupation," she acknowledged softly. She'd been alone for so long, doing whatever the spirit directed, that she'd failed to give what she expected to receive.

"I'd have liked a heads-up," he said. Then added, "Truth is, I want you to take guardianship of Liam as well, but...until now...it's been all me. It might take me a time or two to get used to not being his everything."

Smiling, Priscilla made a note to self to include Jax in every single thing she did with Liam. At least in the beginning. With texts and photos, he could be there with him. Watching his son grow when he couldn't actually be there watching. Then asked, "Do you mind if I take him over to my place tomorrow?"

After a brief pause, he shook his head. "Actually, I don't," he told her. "If you adopt him, he'll be a Fortune, too, and should grow up with that part of his heritage, as well."

Adopt him. The words should have scared the crap out of her. All they did was fill her with a need to squeal. But, thinking from the outside in, she said, "For his sake, we should give the marriage, say, six months, just to make certain I don't drive you crazy or something, and then, I will most definitely be adopting him."

Who'd have thought she didn't have to fall in love and do the whole mucked up relationship thing, to get the dream she'd always wanted? A family of her own.

Different from what others would think when they saw them, but then, so many families looked like one thing on the outside only to be another, less appealing, story underneath.

Her, Jax and Liam…their story was going to be more.

Because she and Jax had the magic key. You married for reasons that mattered to both of you, that *suited* both of you, giving you each something you needed for the future you wanted, not for emotions that were unreliable at best.

Their marriage was going to be built on cement.

Not sinking sand.

Chapter Eight

Jax had to get to bed—the two-hour sprints of rest he got were doable as long as he got a head start on the sleep. If Liam was fussy, or, as had been the case a night or two lately, wide awake, he might end up with no shuteye between one bottle to the next.

But there he sat, empty plate in front of him, nursing the last of his wine. Enjoying the company too much to get up and go to his room. "You said something a bit ago, about finding something your parents had left. What are you looking for?"

Priscilla took on a faraway, somewhat lost expression, before she looked over at him. "That's just it," she told him with a small grin and shrug. "We don't know."

"You're looking for something, but you don't know what it is? Or, presumably where, either, since you have to look?"

She nodded.

"All four of you?" Her brothers and sister were all deeply involved in successful ventures. Surely they didn't have the time to wile away their days on a whim.

"And my Uncle Sander and cousin, too," she said. Leaving Jax more perplexed. He'd grown up on Emerald Ridge with her cousins, the full-time Fortune family, and they all had been…decent, good people. And extremely busy.

He had to ask. "How will you know when you find it?"

Looking him right in the eye, she replied, "We'll know."

By osmosis?

He tried again. "How do you know there's anything to find?"

"My parents were on their way back to us, here, when their plane crashed. Their last communication to us, before boarding the flight, they'd said that they had a surprise here, waiting, and were excited to share it with us."

A little light started to shine on the subject. But… "And you waited all these years to look for it?"

Shaking her head, Priscilla looked over at him, and that time, held his gaze. With something deep and real sparkling from her hazel eyes. Something that seemed to reach inside him and just…be there. "At first, we were all so devastated, no one thought about it. But we've all looked through the years. At various times. When one or the other of us had some time." She sighed. "This summer marked the twentieth anniversary of their deaths. We were all together at the beginning of last month, including my uncle who raised us and was only twenty-four and a widower himself at the time of the crash. Uncle Sander said that it was time we all put our determination and time to working together to find that surprise, no matter what it took. And here we are."

Jax had one thought stick in his brain, front and center, at first. Liam was going to be a lucky young man to be a part of a family like that.

Something he couldn't give his son, with his family's

charred reputation and only him and Annelise left to carry on.

A spot of envy followed.

Until a calculation hit him. "You're twenty-eight," he said, which he already knew. She'd told him the other day.

"Right."

"So you were only eight when your parents died."

She nodded. He'd been the age she was now when he'd lost his mother. And a year older when his dad had died. Empathy filled him. Along with a need to take her in his arms and hold on. To find a cure for the pain she'd suffered so young. For the years of growing up without the kind of support that only a parent—one designed to put the child first—could give.

His parents might not have been deeply in love with each other, but there'd never been a doubt how much they'd both loved Jax and Annelise. And had put their needs first, over and over again as they'd been growing up.

Just as Jax was doing with Liam.

"I'm just so sorry," he finally said, even knowing the words in no way conveyed what he was feeling.

She nodded. "Thank you. But, you know, we had Uncle Sander, and he gave us all a great life. And says that we blessed him fourfold. Which is part of the reason I know that my life will be so well served by this choice we've made. I get to be to Liam what my uncle was to me. The security that set me free to be the best I can be."

Jax blinked. Took a sip of wine and got it down. Knew he had to go up. Didn't want to leave Priscilla sitting all alone.

"Oh! And I have one other errand to run in the morning," Priscilla said, sitting forward, her eyes aglow. "So weird the timing, but today, I was at the Emerald Ridge Café having tea with Harris, and this older woman stops by our table. Vera Duff, you know her?"

"Yeah, she owns the camera shop in town. Has the best of the best if you ever need equipment for anything…"

Shaking her head, Priscilla said, "She's actually selling the place. Which is why she stopped to talk to us. She moved some cabinet and found a pack of negatives that had been lodged behind it. They'd apparently fallen back there and no one knew. Turns out they were of us!"

The glow in the woman's eyes lit Jax up. Replacing some of the sorrow he'd been vicariously suffering with her with something that felt better. "My mom had dropped them off before she left on her trip. Vera didn't know if the negatives had been developed or not. She didn't keep records from that far back, and just plain didn't remember. It's possible that none of us have ever seen these pictures before, and tomorrow morning, I'm stopping by Vera's shop to pick them up. That's another reason I'll have Liam at my place tomorrow. Everyone wants to get a look at the negatives."

Jax figured he should be feeling like an outsider. Or, at the very least, left out. Instead, all he could think was that his son got to be with what was going to be his family during a moving moment in their lives. Not that Liam would remember. But the others might. He'd never been a fanciful guy, but he approved of Liam's presence with the Fortunes in the morning.

And, as hard as it was to believe, in just a couple of days he'd grown comfortable taking on Priscilla Fortune as his wife, too.

A lifetime of cold showers and handshakes, while

promising to be a severe challenge, was a price he was willing to pay.

Jax might be his father's son, with a lot of Henry Wellington's attributes, but, unlike his dad with Courtney, sex wasn't going to be *his* downfall.

Jax had offered to continue to take all of the nighttime feedings while Priscilla got acclimated to her new home, but she'd pulled her *in or out card* again—albeit tongue-in-cheek—to help him see that she was there, willing and needing to jump in.

She'd suggested that they each do two stints in a row, giving the other a full four hours of uninterrupted rest, assuming Liam chose to wake, eat and fall back to sleep on their clocked schedule.

Knowing that Jax had to work, and that he'd spent nearly ten hours doing manual labor in the field that day, Priscilla insisted on taking the midnight and 2:00 a.m. slots, giving Jax a good five hours of uninterrupted rest.

Or would have done had the baby cooperated, in any fashion, with the plan.

Sleepy from the wine she'd consumed, she went to bed early and fell right to sleep. Only to be woken up fifteen minutes later by clearly angry wails. And again forty-five minutes after that. Reminding herself it wasn't her turn for Liam time, and that Jax had been taking care of his baby just fine without her for the past month, she made herself stay in bed.

And got back to sleep, too.

Until she was abruptly pulled from a dream she couldn't remember by a loud scream that didn't stop.

Sitting up, Priscilla glanced at the door between her room and the nursery, and then at the clock.

Eleven forty-five? She'd overslept.

And Liam was up fifteen minutes early.

Reaching for the robe she'd left at the end of her bed, pulling it on over the matching silk shorty pajamas she generally wore to bed, she was through the nursery door before she had the silk belt tied. Stumbling toward the crib, she stopped as her eyes adjusted to the dim lighting.

Jax was there, in nothing but a pair of gym shorts, reaching for a diaper. That's when she noticed that the door to his room was also open.

"I'm sorry," she said, loudly enough to be heard over the crying, hating that she'd failed on her very first shift. "I just heard him. I'll take it from here." She reached for the baby.

Laying the squalling infant on the changing table, Jax said, "You don't want this one."

Two seconds later she caught a whiff that clued her in. And as his diaper came fully undone, Liam quieted. "I could have handled it just fine," she insisted, standing back just a foot from the table. She'd changed plenty of dirty diapers during her volunteering stints at the women's shelter nursery.

And...well... Liam had done quite the duty. "He needs a bath," she said, walking toward the door. "I'll get it going." Heading across the hall to the bathroom that had been designated as Liam's—and had a kneeling mat on the floor and installed baby tub in the bath. She'd been given the rundown of where everything was on her tour of the home the day before. Grabbing a couple of clean, soft baby washcloths, she had the water set to the perfect tepid temperature as Jax entered the roomy space and set the naked baby in the padded safety ring that would help hold him upright as Priscilla bathed him.

Liam didn't scream as he hit the water, but he fussed through the entire bath. A process that Priscilla handled well enough, but not as proficiently as Jax might have done. She felt him behind her, watching, making her tense, like she was on trial and expecting a guilty verdict.

"This is a first," she admitted, in case he hadn't been able to tell. "I watched videos last night and this morning."

"He's getting clean, that's what matters," Jax said.

She'd been holding Liam's arm, but it slipped through her soapy fingers. Thankfully the ring loosely circling the little body kept the baby upright for the second it took her to correct her error, and she made it through the rest of the process without embarrassment. With splotches of wet silk sticking to her, she lifted the baby and held him up while Jax put a terry-cloth hood over Liam's head and wrapped him up in the rest of the towel.

Jax got the baby lotioned and diapered, and then moved aside as Priscilla held up the clean sleeper she'd brought from a drawer full of them. Liam was starting to fuss again, and she made quick work of getting ahold of flying feet and squirming arms and sliding them into their appropriate sleeves and spots. She zipped the one-piece outfit and lifted Liam, cradling him in one arm, turning, to see Jax pulling a bottle out of the warmer.

"I can take it from here," she told him, welcoming the silence as, bottle in hand, she presented the nipple and Liam latched on hungrily. The rocker welcomed her with padding under her butt and at her back, and it was only as Liam's eyes closed while he drank hungrily that she glanced up to see Jax still standing there.

Staring. She thought, at first, that it was his son that had his attention. Until she noticed he was glancing more to her right side than the left where Liam lay.

That's when she realized that her right breast was molded as though it was nude by the clinging wet spot of silk positioned over half of it.

Pretending not to be aware of his attention blip, she murmured, "You should get back to sleep." And kept her gaze focused wholly on the infant who was already starting to breathe deeply. Evenly. As though sleep was only a minute or two away.

"I never went to sleep," Jax said, letting her know he was still there. And close. "He hasn't gone down either yet…"

At which her shocked gaze shot up at him. "What? I heard him earlier, but…not for a few hours…"

Leaning a shoulder against the doorjamb between his room and the nursery, Jax said, "I took him downstairs for a while."

So she could sleep? And she'd done so, blissfully unaware that he'd been up tending to the baby she'd promised to mother. Colossal fail. But… "Has he ever done that before? Been up for what, four hours straight? And did he eat?"

Glancing down, she saw Liam's little lips diligently at work, while his little throat seemed to be swallowing as though he hadn't eaten in days.

"He wouldn't take his bottle," Jax said. "Which was a first. He didn't want to be in his swing. Walking him didn't make a difference. But pooping finally did. I'm guessing he had a gassy stomach."

Good. Poop talk. Deleted any hint of desire over recent breast awareness.

"And yes, he had a similar bout once before I was on full-time duty. I was told about it afterward."

"Christa handled that one?" she guessed, not wanting him, or Liam to feel awkward using the other woman's name. Priscilla had no reason to feel jealous, ever, where Jax was concerned. And the woman had given birth to Liam. She would be honored for that role in perpetuity as far as Priscilla was concerned.

"No," Jax's answer surprised her. As did the fact that he was still standing there. Watching. But not as though he was checking up on her ability to feed his son. More like he was just sharing the moment.

A ridiculous thought popping in out of nowhere. Priscilla brushed it off as Jax said, "The Noveltys had him. I was at a fundraiser, and Christa had…gone out. I didn't know that until I'd returned."

Priscilla had a flash of memory. Something he'd said at the beginning of the week. About Christa not being alone when she'd died. And realized that while Jax, by his own admission, hadn't loved his wife, he'd still been hurt by her infidelity after they'd married.

She remembered hearing something about his father maybe stepping out on his mother. Years ago. One summer. Priscilla had been sixteen, seventeen maybe. There'd been rumors…

"I meant it when I told you I won't ever be unfaithful to our marriage, Jax," she said softly, noticing that Liam, while still sucking softly, had grown heavy with sleep.

"I know without us being intimate with each other that we're asking a lot of each other, but I'm not going to put you through that. It's disrespectful to you, but also to myself and to both our family names." She felt the truth of her words to her core.

He nodded. Hadn't moved from his position by the door. And she was going to have to get up. The silky belt on her robe had loosened and was going to fall open. But Liam needed to be put in his crib shortly after he fell asleep, or she risked waking him when she laid him down.

An insight gleaned from Sasha, but one she'd also learned through personal experience that morning.

Being a new mother, she did what she had to do. Stood, walked with the gaping open robe to the crib, laid the baby gently on his back, and then straightened. Deliberately turning her back on Jax, she headed toward her own door.

Wrapping her lips around some kind of "good night, sleep tight" to offer generically to the both of them as she reached her door, she stopped when she heard Jax's softly uttered, "Would you join me in another glass of wine to assist in the falling asleep process?"

Her body wanted to spin. To accept. But her mind kept her rooted to her spot on the floor.

"We need to talk, Priscilla."

Those words, known to so many as breakup words, sent her mood spiraling downward, while her half-formed excuse to decline flew out the window.

Was he about to tell her that it wasn't working out for him? But they were barely getting started. Hadn't had a chance to acclimate yet, even. So much was at stake. And… Priscilla felt like she'd actually found her life's purpose.

And she was providing a way for Jax to have what he most wanted and needed, too. Security for his son and their life together.

But he could take his chances in court, too. Had a possibility of winning full custody. Without any sacrifice at all.

With a nod, she tightened the belt on her robe, spun a half turn, squared her shoulders and headed out through the nursery door into the hallway.

Wondering how she was going to convince Jax Wellington to give them more time.

And if it was even right to try.

Chapter Nine

Jax was halfway across the hall when he realized that Priscilla was headed for the stairs. "In here," he called softly, motioning to the door directly across from their suite of rooms. "This used to be my mother's reading room," he told her as he crossed the lightly colored, expensively sewn floral design carpet to the marble countertop that ran along one wall. "This was Annelise's wing of the house. Courtney never came up here, and my sister kept the room pretty much as our mother left it."

The home was going to be hers. She should know its history. "Now that you're the woman of the house, you should make this room your own. Do whatever you want to it. New carpet, furniture…whatever."

Turning from the wine he was about to pour, he saw Priscilla standing in the doorway. "This door was closed when you showed me the house," she said. "I thought it was storage."

"Annelise's things were still in here. She'd told me to have them packed up, and I'd done so, but left everything in here—figuring they could wait until she got back from her trip overseas. I had it cleaned out this afternoon when the construction was being done."

Standing there barefoot—in the gym shorts he'd started

to sleep in the night before since there was a lady living in the wing with them—Jax held out the glass of wine he'd just poured. He saw Priscilla hesitate there in the doorway before slowly heading toward him. She'd tied the belt on her robe into a bow.

He noticed that, and everything else about her womanly curves as she approached. The wet boob was covered. He had mixed reactions to that one. Relief. Disappointment.

"Here's to making it work," he said, toasting her with a tap of his glass to hers. He was tired. Had just come off the most frustrating four hours of fatherhood yet. And was facing a lifetime of no sex.

And sentencing her to the same.

He watched her sip as hesitantly as she'd joined him, and saw her eyes dip lower, too. No way she wasn't going to note his very masculine reaction to her. It had been pretty obvious since the moment he'd noticed the most exquisite silk plastered breast.

"So yeah," he said, dropping his butt to the arm of an overstuffed floral couch as he took a second sip of wine. "We failed to consider the effect of living in close quarters with each other, day in and day out, while at the same time being ruled by abstinence, both inside and outside the home."

Holding her wineglass in front of her with both hands, which had her forearms covering her breasts, Priscilla asked, "That's what you wanted to talk about?"

She sounded surprised. Which actually got his mind on something beside her delectable body for a very welcome second. "Yeah. What did you think it was about?"

His misstep in the nursery had been fairly obvious.

Hell, Liam would probably have called him on it with an assertive wail if the little guy had been awake.

"I…" She glanced at her wine, then at Jax over the rim of her glass. "I thought you were having second thoughts about us getting married."

He had been. Because of the hard-on. But had been quickly struck by how wrong it would be to give up his son's best shot because Jax couldn't keep it in his pants.

He could. And would.

If he had to.

"I think that ship has sailed," he said, looking her right in the eye. "For all the reasons we've both been over. This marriage feels right to me. Like it's the best choice for many reasons. And from what you've said, you're experiencing the same kind of confidence."

She nodded. Held his gaze. His hard-on became enlarged. The elephant in the room.

Glancing down at his crotch, he said, "We need to talk about it."

She shrugged. Sipped. Watched him. "So talk."

She was good, he'd give her that. A match for him. Not what he'd been expecting.

Some shyness, aversion, even a come on he'd been prepared to handle. But handing the situation back to him? Taking another sip of wine, he nodded. Considered his next words. Or would have if there'd been any. He was coming up empty. Until something she'd said earlier, a day or two ago, hit him. Trust was the basis of their future.

"Honestly, I'm not sure what to say, other than that it's an issue," he told her. "It's a natural occurrence. It's going to happen. And while in most circumstances it wouldn't be obvious, with us living in such close quarters, sharing a nursery with a baby that doesn't plan his needs to our schedules, or even give us much of heads-up on what he might require at any given moment, it's going to be a part of our relationship."

The way she sucked in her lip at that aroused him further. He'd never just lost himself without some kind of actual physical stimulation, but Jax was growing concerned that it could happen. Right there.

He'd prefer to avoid that extreme embarrassment.

"It is?" Priscilla's voice sounded strained.

The two words confused him. Until he replayed his own words of seconds before. *It's going to be a part of our relationship.* What the hell. Was she enjoying his discomfort?

"I'd say the obviousness of that one has already presented itself."

"The only thing obvious here is that you saw something that turned you on," she said then, a strange glimmer in her eyes. "Not that us doing something about it is going to be a part of our relationship."

Confused for a second, Jax frowned. And then was hit by the "it." The one that he'd so emphatically stated was going to be a part of them. Had she thought he meant sex? As in, them having it?

"I was referring to sexual desire rearing its head now and then between us. Like it did tonight when I looked up and saw—"

"We both know what you saw," Priscilla said, cutting him off. "So...what are you proposing we do about it?"

The woman was giving him nothing. Was she open

to a mutually satisfying physical relationship as it suited their living together status, within the grounds of no affairs being tolerated? Or just not understanding how uncomfortable he felt at the moment? And would be feeling for the entirety of the foreseeable future.

Not that it was her problem.

Nor did he in any way see it as her responsibility to ease his discomfort. Big period on that one.

But… "I don't know what to propose until I know where you stand on the whole desire thing. Is it something you see yourself experiencing? Or am I the only one?"

Priscilla coughed. Half-choked was more like it. And then gulped wine. Suddenly lightening Jax's mood. A lot.

"I'll take that as a you can envision yourself in the same boat I'm currently sinking in," he said gruffly.

With a tilt of her head, she gave him the acknowledgment he'd hoped to receive. And not because he wanted a partner in agony. Or an excuse to diffuse the suffering. "So we're on even ground here as we enter the discussion," he said aloud.

"We're *just* entering it?" she asked, finally moving to sit on the opposite end of the couch on which he was perched. "I was kind of hoping we'd just had it."

He felt her pain. "You think it's smart to leave an open flame by a can of gasoline?"

"So what do you propose? That I move to the other wing of the house? Because that's not going to work, Jax. We'd have to take every other night, moving Liam every day, and that's just not…"

Her words trailed off as he shook his head. And then answered her question. "I'm not proposing anything," he told her. "Just needing to get it out in the open. We play it day by day, I guess. Being honest with each other. And if there comes a time when it's less painful to…maybe… give each other some relief now and then, it would be a mutual decision knowing that our choice is based on logic, physical facts of nature and us tending to the health of our relationship. Not stemming from some undying love that is drawing us together."

As it turned out, he'd had the words right there. For him, anyway.

Watching Priscilla, he wasn't so sure. Until her gaze narrowed, and she said, "If that time comes, we'll both be on the same page about that," she assured him. And then stood, crossing to the counter to put her half-full glass down. "In the meantime, we need to get some sleep. My two hours are dwindling, and you haven't had any rest at all…"

Finishing off the wine in his glass, praying it helped him get to sleep in spite of his aroused state, Jax set his glass next to hers and walked behind her to the door. And thought to say, "Don't panic if Liam doesn't wake up on schedule. Last time he had a bout like this he slept through two feedings. I ended up waking him up because I thought something was wrong with him."

She looked at him over her shoulder. "I'm guessing he wasn't happy about that," she said, grinning, and nearly walked into the door frame.

Jax reached for her, wrapping an arm around her upper torso to pull her away, and ended up with her backside against his front side.

His hips thrust forward, then he stilled. Jax steadied

Priscilla and then let go as though he'd been burned. Snapping back and staying clear.

Priscilla wasn't as quick to react. She stood rooted to the spot for a couple of long seconds, and then headed out to the hallway. Following behind her, Jax vowed to never enter that reading room again, even as he knew the thought was ridiculous. It was all he had. A promise to himself. As though if he never stepped on the floral carpet, he'd never get hard for his soon to be wife, either.

He was so busy talking to himself, he missed that Priscilla had stopped again. Turning to face him. He caught on, too late to stop his forward momentum that had his body up against hers for a second time.

Mouth open, she just stood there, looking up at him.

And, God help him, Jax had no more rational fight left in him. Seeing those full, parted lips, the hazel eyes peering up at him, seemingly filled with question, he had no other choice but to provide the answer.

His head lowered slowly. There was time for her to turn her head. To back away. But when his mouth reached the touching zone, she was still there.

Calling out to him with her readiness for more.

And so he gave it to her.

Priscilla didn't think. Desire mixed with heady doses of admiration, affection and excitement for the future, even some gratitude all converged upon her. Driving her to wrap her arms around Jax's neck as, their lips joined, he lifted her and carried her to the bed she'd climbed out of less than an hour before.

She didn't question the untying of her robe, or process ramifications when his nearly naked body came down with her scantily clad one as they hit her mattress and her robe fell to the floor. There was no awareness of the future, of anything but the want that was raging between two people who'd vowed to spend the rest of their lives together.

His hands slid up under her short silk spaghetti strap top to find her breasts and she moaned, lifting her tightened nipples into his palms, feeling an answering fire between her legs as first his hands then his thumbs moved along the tips of her simultaneously.

Propelled by sensation, she reached downward, sliding her hand inside the elastic waistband of his shorts, thrilling as she met unfettered eager flesh reaching toward her. She encircled him. Holding on. Taking some kind of primitive possession.

His hands left her breasts, moving to her shorts and yanked downward, exposing the chill of night air to her hot skin.

Her legs spread because they had to, and as he nudged one knee and then the other, climbing between her thighs, she pulled his shorts out of the way.

He entered her in one thrust. Filling her. Driving her to the brink so that when he pulled back and pushed forward again, her body convulsed around him. Pulling his seed out of him and into her.

Coming down wasn't as quick. Priscilla lay there, warm beneath him. Tingling. Breathing. Floating. Until… suddenly there was no warmth. No him.

Just cold air on her skin. Jax lay next to her for a moment. He turned, planted his lips on hers, and she welcomed them. Feeling the joining like some kind of promise.

She was drowsy. Content. Ready to sleep.

Until the bed moved again, waking her fully in time to see Jax's back as he headed into the hallway.

Priscilla lay there with the sex still an entity in her bed. Blaming no one. Not sorry it had happened. Not all that happy about it, either.

Mostly, the only awareness washing over her, through her, was that she'd never felt as alone as she did right then.

Jax blamed the wine. Swore off it. He showered, went to bed, and forced himself to clear his mind and sleep. Something he'd always been good at. Letting go.

He woke when Liam did, some three hours after they'd put him down. Closed his mind to the woman in silk tending to his son. And went back to sleep.

By morning, he was ready for frank conversation. In jeans, a long-sleeved plaid cotton shirt and cowboy boots, he found Priscilla in the garden room downstairs, in flattering navy pants and a cropped navy-and-white top that drew his attention straight to her breasts.

Instant memories flashed before his eyes. The slightly darkened color of her nipples, their hardness in contrast to the soft, cushioning flesh they topped.

Liam. Forcing his mind away from temptation and back to the reason Priscilla Fortune was in his house, lounging on the couch reading. His son's swing clicked softly as it moved back and forth, rocking the baby while he slept.

Priscilla's hazel eyes lifted toward him, her gaze holding his.

"I'd apologize," he told her. "Except that it was clearly mutual."

Lips pursing she nodded. He took an easier breath. As

long as they could face things realistically, be logical and stay on the same page, they'd get through the rocky parts. He was hanging his son's future on the belief.

Almost immediately, though…with a glance at Liam… he got tense all over again. He and Priscilla could agree all they wanted, and still end up with situations that neither of them had signed on for.

And then what?

"We didn't use protection." He'd refused to let himself dwell on the fact the night before. Nothing he could do about it after the fact, and with a long day of fencing ahead of him, he'd had to get some rest.

"I just came off my cycle. And run like clockwork." She spoke pragmatically. As though discussing her most intimate bodily functions was commonplace. For her, they could be. Yet he didn't think so. And took the conversation as another plus—they'd arrived at a place where they could share things with each other that they didn't share with others.

But then, their whole relationship was that. The big secret that had brought them together—the fake marriage that wasn't going to be fake at all—just not a love match.

Assuming she was still on board. Which was why he'd sought her out. Still standing straight in the doorway, not even stepping one foot into the room, he asked, "Are you still okay with moving forward with our plans?"

Her glance was piercing. "Are you?"

He didn't hesitate. "I am."

"Then I am, too."

Good, and just to get on with it then, so they didn't have to continually revisit their pact, he said, "We should set a date. Soon."

"We have to go to town together to get the license. Tell me when you want to do that and I'll be ready. As long as it's not this morning."

Right, she had plans. Potentially big ones. And he'd been so filled with his own drama that he'd failed to remember that she had a full life, some of it outside him and Liam. And that that life mattered every bit as much as Wellington Ranch. Though, she was planning to take his son along with her to get her photos—and to look for the big surprise. Because Liam was going to be a part of that family, too.

"How about Monday?" Jax asked. Needing it done. Wanting it done.

"Monday's good," she said. "I don't think we need an appointment. Generally clerks can handle that paperwork. We'd just need to set a time with the judge to actually marry us and certify the union as legal. The license is good for like three months, so we have time to figure out that part."

He nodded. Had just been through the process. His expression must have said something to that effect as she then said, "Which you already know since you just went through it."

His second marriage in a year. Seemed about right for a Wellington. His father's direct descendent. "The license is valid three days after issue date, and for eighty-nine days total. That ninetieth day, you start the process over again." He'd been through that, too.

"I take it you and Christa didn't get it done in the eighty-nine days?"

"She had some doubts," he said, leaning his shoulder against the doorjamb. "Considering that the union was only taking place because of the baby, with both of us knowing it wouldn't have happened if not for the fact that she was pregnant, I understood. Now, I'm thinking she'd already hooked up with the guy she was with the day she died."

Made it easier for him to think that, somehow. That Christa had at least been confident that Jax would make a good husband and father—just that she'd wanted love, too. He didn't blame her for that.

But as she stood there, hearing his words, he saw a pattern. "Kind of like we're doing, huh?" He had to get it out there. Trust. Honesty. The only way they were going to work. "Only getting married because of Liam…it wouldn't be happening if not for him…"

With a quirk of her lips, she asked, "You getting cold feet on me, Wellington?"

And Jax smiled. Priscilla Fortune and Christa Novelty were two very, very different women. And there was no doubt in his mind which one was better suited to him. Beyond that, the one date they'd had…their time together since…had been far more intriguing with Priscilla than it had ever been with his wife. "More like in need of a cold shower," he told her. "And I'll make sure they happen in time from now on."

The words were his parting shot. He issued them, then turned to head out to the tasks that, while physically taxing, he knew he could master.

He was halfway down the hall when Pricilla's voice reached him. He didn't stop. Wasn't even sure she'd been talking to him. Could be Liam had just opened his eyes.

Could be. But he didn't think so.

No reason for her to have said, "Or not," to a waking infant.

They'd been meant for him.

And stuck with him persistently for the rest of the morning.

Chapter Ten

Priscilla hadn't slept much. Enough to get by, but she figured a nap on her own couch was on the docket during Liam's afternoon snooze. Heading out into the day with a smile on her face.

Jax was… Jax. He didn't believe in love—but loved deeply. His dedication to his son was proof positive of that. He also didn't believe in marriage, but was committed to theirs. As she drove into town, with Liam sleeping strapped securely in his infant car seat behind her, she replayed her conversation with Jax that morning. And came out with one very clear conclusion.

He'd been worried that their activity the night before had changed her mind about marrying him. And had clearly been relieved when he'd found that it hadn't.

Because of Liam. She got that. But she, too, was there because of the precious baby she kept glancing at through the rearview mirror. So hard to believe that in just a few short days her life had changed so drastically, giving her a deeper sense of purpose in addition to her pursuits outside the home.

And if, as adults, they ended up filling other needs for each other, to keep them happy in their marriage, then they did.

Would she have liked the experience better if Jax had stayed with her in bed afterward? Most definitely. But life wasn't perfect.

A lesson she'd learned harshly the day her parents' plane had crashed. But that eight-year-old kid had grown up well loved. Happy. You just had to roll with the punches.

And so she rolled into town, unlatched the baby carrier from the car seat as she'd learned to do the day before, to lug the thing proudly looped over her arm as she and her soon to be son headed inside Emerald Ridge Camera and Photo.

Vera was alone in the shop, and, glancing up as Priscilla came in the door, the woman grabbed a big envelope off the counter and came toward her. "There are hundreds of negatives in here," she said, frowning. "I wish I'd kept past records. I just don't have any way of knowing if your mother ever got developed photos. We know she dropped these off, because they're here, but if they fell behind the counter and then she didn't come back to collect them, it's possible that the photos she ordered were never made."

Priscilla's hand was shaking as she took the envelope. And noticed, first thing, the date on it. "This was just a couple of weeks before Mom and Dad were killed," she said softly. Almost reverently. Feeling lightheaded for a second as she stood there, touching an envelope her mother had last touched, while holding an infant that was soon going to make her a mother. Like past and present, human and spiritual were all colliding right then, in that very spot.

"I'm so sorry," Vera said, pulling Priscilla out of her time warp and back into the present. With a heart that seemed to have grown exponentially, she was there. The same woman, on the same errand, and yet…felt changed. Different.

"Don't be sorry…" Priscilla found words, and met the older woman's gaze. "You have no idea what a gift these will be to me and my family if they're photos we've never seen before…"

She had to get to the estate. Everyone was planning to gather in the main house at ten. To see the negatives, and then, those who had the time would be searching for the surprise. They were covering the entire compound, one piece at a time.

As it turned out, Priscilla couldn't make it to the big house. Liam woke up, needing to be changed and fed, and then didn't want to go right back to sleep. Putting him in his swing, the one thing she'd discovered that seemed to comfort the little guy when he was cranky, she called up to the house and asked everyone to meet her at her cottage instead.

It felt right that she, soon to be a married woman, be the hostess for the others. Not just the youngest, with no career or solid purpose, who could always be available anytime, anywhere, any of them called on her. Her life was changing, and she was becoming more as a result. Stronger. Feeling more confident.

Realizing for the first time that while her family would always be a major component in her world, she also had a life outside of their fold.

She had the envelope open, in the middle of the table when everyone arrived. She hadn't yet looked inside, or pulled anything out. The moment belonged to all of them, not just her. She'd expected them all to circle the table, and then had envisioned Uncle Sander actually reaching for the negatives and spreading them out among them all.

Much like he'd served up dinner plates all those years when Linc's mother would put the serving platters on the tray beside him. Or how he'd always passed out Christmas gifts from under the tree, making certain that they all went in order so that no one, including Linc, got left out. The thought brought a pang of sorrow for the young man who'd grown up among them and then lost his way. And dying so young.

But while Priscilla stood at the table, reflecting, the rest of her family gathered around the baby swing. Oohing and ahhing. As though Priscilla had actually just given birth to the little one slated to be the newest member of their family. Roth, only just becoming a new father himself, was the first one to pick up Liam, holding him carefully as he talked gibberish to him.

Wide-eyed, the baby stared up at him, and then, one by one, each of her siblings, her uncle and her cousin, all took turns with the baby, while Priscilla looked on, smiling.

And trying not to cry.

Wishing that she'd known…that she'd waited to introduce her family to Liam when Jax was there, to witness and share in his son's welcome into the Fortune clan.

Taking out her phone, she took a quick video. Got them all in. And had the camera shut off before anyone knew what she'd done. She was being goofy, she knew.

But…you rolled with punches, and you also memorialized the moments that meant the most. As their parents had with their old-fashioned camera that required film and developing before one actually got to view the memories.

Uncle Sander was holding Liam as the crew made its

way to the table. Roth and Harris at one end, Uncle Sander at the other, with Priscilla, Zara and Kelsey taking up the sides. Handing Liam to Kelsey, who'd been vocal in her impatience to have her turn, Sander grabbed the envelope, turned it on an angle and pulled back, leaving a trail of negatives along the table.

A trail that Priscilla knew would be with her for the rest of her life. From a day she would never forget. Twenty years after her parents' deaths, she had them back. With hundreds of pieces of evidence of the times, and the love, they'd all shared. No one had seen any of the pictures before, but most of them burst into tales they had to tell when they saw them. Roth and Sander remembered most.

She had tears in her eyes when Uncle Sander said, "I wonder if Marlene took these in to have made into photos for the hallway wall."

Kelsey, handing a sleeping Liam back to Priscilla right when she needed the snuggly warmth the most, said, "It makes sense."

And everyone else around the table nodded. Each in their own world for a second, their own memories. And yet, all them together, filling Priscilla's cottage with the love that would never die. Love that was gifted to them by Marlene and Mark Fortune.

A love that Priscilla was going to make certain that Liam felt every day of his life.

The negatives would be developed. They were all going to get copies of the photos. And Priscilla figured one of the first things she was going to do was make a family photo wall right there in cottage. And include portraits of the Wellingtons, too. The ones that Jax wanted to remember.

And if the future was kind, there'd be more photos taken, more memories made, of Liam growing up. Of their family of three sharing happy times, even if she and Jax weren't in love.

If the future was kind, she'd have her own family memorabilia to add to the rest.

If the future was kind.

Jax didn't trust the future. It brought curveballs that changed life irrevocably, and over which he had no control. For himself, he'd long since stopped worrying about the challenges that were on his path forward. He'd take them on, just as he always had. And adjust accordingly.

But he wasn't just planning for himself anymore. He had Liam to consider. A son who was completely dependent and helpless. One who'd have no way to fight for his needs. His wants. His rights. Since the day the baby had been born, Jax had been uneasy with the knowledge. Needing to conquer it, but not knowing how.

Until Priscilla.

Sitting with her that afternoon, it all became clear to him.

She'd texted to tell him that she and Liam were back, but that Sasha had called saying she wasn't feeling well, and Jax had knocked off early to come relieve her of baby duty for a bit. For all he knew she had plans to help out at the animal shelter. Or read to patients at the hospital, like she had with Emma Novelty's mean Uncle Edrick.

No way he wanted to be responsible for her missing a session. That one day of volunteer reading had helped far more than Uncle Edrick. It had helped solidify Priscilla with the Noveltys as a candidate for Liam's stepmother. And had given him two of the best farm dogs he'd ever known.

As it had turned out, she not only hadn't had plans, but had been full of things to share with him. Starting with how great Liam had been in the car, falling asleep each time the car started and not waking until it stopped. He'd hated to tell her that he'd already discovered that piece of information himself, as he did take his son into town on a regular basis. But just smiled as she continued rattling on, getting it all out in a hurry, as he'd come to know was her way.

While Liam ate and nodded off in Jax's arms, she talked about the negatives she'd picked up that morning, blowing out memory after memory. Filling the room with her smiles, some sadness, but most of all gallons and gallons of love. All of which had been poured into them through her parents and the life they'd given their children.

Then she pulled out her phone. Showing him the video she'd taken that morning in her cottage on the Emerald Ridge River—a cottage he'd never even seen—with his son the star of the show. Yet all of the Fortunes he knew by sight and name, fawning over Liam as one of their own.

He could hardly take it all in, saw logically what was in front of him, but couldn't comprehend, emotionally, exactly how it all worked. He'd had good times with his dad growing up. And with his mom. Separately. But when they'd been together as a family, there'd been no gathering anything like what he was viewing on Priscilla's phone. The vying for turns to hold Liam, the teasing, the love they were lavishing on his son…it was all new.

There'd been kindness in his home. Or at the very

least, politeness. There'd never been hurled accusations, violence, or even much anger, that he could remember. There'd just never been…warmth. Not that he'd felt. Annelise maybe had. She'd been the baby girl. Treated with kid gloves. But it hadn't been just him who'd missed out. At least not from his perspective. He'd never noticed affection expressed between his parents, either. It just hadn't been their way.

What he'd been shown, and so taught, while growing up, was…a sense of family…from a distance. Or *with* distance.

Sitting in the rocking chair in Liam's nursery, looking at that phone while Priscilla leaned against the changing table, bubbling over with the wealth the day had brought her, it hit him. The only way for him to be at peace with whatever might come was to make certain that he provided for Liam. And he wanted his son to have the same type of childhood memories that had shaped Liam's soon to be stepmother.

The fact that Priscilla had agreed to marry him, meant more in that moment than anything ever had in his life. Even if he screwed up—as he would now and then—she'd be there, with her family, to show Liam a better way.

Standing abruptly, he handed Priscilla her phone, set down the bottle his son had emptied before falling asleep, and said, "Let's go now. The court office is open until five. We can get the license today, since we're both free, and not have to make a special trip into town on Monday." There he was, always coming up with logical justification for anything he wanted to do.

As though he couldn't admit to himself that he didn't want to wait even another two days?

Before Priscilla could even pocket her phone, let alone reply, he continued with, "As we've just established, he sleeps fine in the car, and he's newly changed and fed, so we can probably even squeeze in some dinner before we head back."

The three of them, out to dinner as a family...yes, a good plan. Collecting more witnesses to the family bond Jax was forming around his son.

He wanted to believe being seen out and about was the reason he'd made the offer. But had vowed to be honest. Something he couldn't offer to Priscilla if he was lying to himself.

And so, as they headed out to her car—as it had the new car seat and his was in his truck—he climbed behind the steering wheel when she offered, and admitted, to himself, that he was glad to be there.

With her.

Turned out, getting a marriage license wasn't all that big of a deal. Less consuming than getting a driver's license, Priscilla thought, leaving the courthouse that afternoon.

With a driver's license, the second she'd had the temporary permit, she'd been allowed to drive—albeit with restrictions. But still, she slid in behind the wheel and operated the vehicle. But the piece of paper she and Jax had been granted meant absolutely nothing for three days.

And then nothing after that, too, if they didn't actually get married. It would just fade into oblivion as if it had never been.

Which meant there was absolutely no reason for the excitement coursing through her, the deeper purpose to her step, or the warmth invading her heart, either. And yet, it was all there. Almost alarmingly so.

She got the *warmth* where Liam was concerned. Loving the baby was part of her new job description. But when it came to his father?

No way could she allow herself to believe that she was falling in love with Jax Wellington. She could be fond of him. Grateful to him. She could admire him, enjoy time spent in his company and even want sex with him. But she could *not* fall for him.

Doing so would ruin everything. Her emotions would interfere with logic. Would become part of the mix in every choice she made. Would control her.

Control. The word hit her hard as she showered Saturday morning. She'd stepped under the spray with two goals in mind. Clean her body, and her mind. And then she'd step out into the new day with a much clearer perspective than she'd had going to bed Friday night.

With the trip to the courthouse, the dinner, and her lack of sleep Thursday night or a nap thereafter, she'd been more susceptible than usual. Had even cried a little when Jax hadn't opened her bedroom door and joined her after his last turn feeding Liam. She'd somehow figured his having done so would have put the perfect exclamation point to the once in lifetime evening they'd shared in town.

Assuming one only got one marriage license in a lifetime, and celebrated it with their baby afterward.

Priscilla had never consciously thought much about the way she ran her life. She just did what her inner self prompted her to do. Trusted herself to do her best and lead her right.

But…control? Was that what it had all been about? The reason she was still just volunteering, helping others—in plural, all over, not just one place—creating no life for herself? Until that week.

Because she'd had to be in charge, and giving one's heart to others—outside the family you were born to which wasn't a choice—gave up a semblance of that autonomy. Because it gave someone else the ability to hurt you. To break your heart.

As her eight-year-old heart had been broken.

Seeing those pictures the day before—some that were taken just before her parents had left on their trip—had been a blessing. A wonderful gift.

And crushing, too. She'd survived, blossomed, been happy…because from that day forward, she hadn't allowed herself to risk getting hurt.

Liam had broken through the twenty-year-old walls she'd subconsciously built. It was as though he'd been placed in her path on purpose. He'd touched her deepest heart.

Turning off the water falling upon her, Priscilla grabbed a towel, wrapped herself in it and slid down to marble tile on the bathroom floor, knees to her chest. And shook.

Liam was one thing. Loving a child was different. You knew going in you had to let go. You raised them and set them free to go out into the world without you. To make their own lives, their own way.

But beyond that, no.

Just no.

She couldn't fall in love with Jax.

She *could not*.

And so she wouldn't. The thought presented itself so calmly, she hardly felt its impact at first. But then it was everywhere. Standing, she nodded at herself in the mirror. She was in control of her own thoughts. Her own choices. Her own life.

And so she would not fall in love with Jax.

It was just that simple.

She'd made her choice.

And it was the right one for her.

Chapter Eleven

Jax was out evaluating fence line on Saturday, midmorning, when he got a text from Priscilla. He'd assigned a clip of an old rock tune to her number, so that he'd always know it was her when she tried to reach him. Pulling his horse to a stop, he grabbed his phone from his pocket and read.

The Noveltys are here.

Just that, nothing else. No alarm signal. Or even a polite request for him to return. With a yank of the reins, he'd turned around and was galloping back full speed before he'd dropped his phone back into his shirt pocket.

The Noveltys had been to Wellington Ranch several times. He'd told them they were always welcome to visit their grandson. They'd never once shown up unannounced.

His ex-in-laws were checking up on him. Jax's attempts to get witnesses to his new romantic union had obviously reached them, and they were paying a surprise visit to see if it was all show, or the real thing. He'd half expected as much.

They didn't trust Jax. He didn't totally blame them for

that. He'd slept with their daughter without having any deep feelings for her. Didn't matter that she'd never had any for him, either. Why Christa had thought it important to share the fact with her parents that Jax had been about to break up with her when she'd told him she was pregnant, he could only guess.

But he figured he knew. She'd been paving the way into the future when she was going to divorce Jax and come out about her rekindled love affair with the man she'd been serious with before her fling with Jax.

He'd been a rebound. Overall, he was fine with that.

Just not when it came to the Noveltys thinking that Liam was a fling, too. Something he was into only for the moment. While it was new and exciting.

He'd never been more committed to anything in his life.

Tethering his horse close to the mansion, Jax stopped inside the mudroom to wash up, and then sauntered into the house as though he was there of his own accord. Making one of his usual stop-ins to see his son. Something he hadn't done in the few days that Priscilla had been there.

It was only as he was approaching the garden room—clearly Priscilla's favorite—from which he heard voices, that it dawned on him that he should have given her a heads-up regarding his presence. Stopping in his tracks in the hallway, he stood, realizing that, unlike other visits, Liam wasn't the only one the Noveltys had come to see that day. They were going to be watching Jax and Priscilla, too.

He had no idea if she was ready to put on a show. Or even if she was willing. He'd seen the invitation in her expression last night when she'd headed from the nursery into her room. Those hazel eyes had been so open, so honest, and he'd been unable to look away.

Which was why he hadn't opened the door she'd closed behind her.

And other than a few texts that morning, to coordinate her tending to Liam while Jax was at work, they hadn't spoken since.

He'd found coffee on when he'd headed downstairs to the kitchen, but that was as likely to have been Sasha's doing, as anything else.

Should he just go in? Play things naturally? And have Priscilla pull back when he bent in to kiss her hello?

Or give her a heads-up? Which might end up being overkill and alert the Noveltys to the personal awkwardness between him and his intended.

"Jax, is that you?" Priscilla's voice reached him while he stood there vacillating.

"Yeah!" he called out cheerfully, plastering a grin on his face as he headed the last few steps down the hall and into the room. How in the hell Priscilla had known he was there, he couldn't fathom, but he hoped it was a good sign that she'd called out to him. She'd sounded friendly.

Indicating her readiness to play along?

With a greeting of a light peck on her lips running through his mind, Jax was about to find out.

Priscilla had been watching through the window for Jax ever since she'd texted him. As he had every time he left the house, he'd messaged her where he was going to be that morning. She'd positioned herself in the garden room to be able to see that horizon. And had been watching for a sign of horse and rider. Breathing a huge sigh of relief when they'd briefly come into view.

And had been listening for his boots on the tile floor ever since. A sound she'd already learned in just the few days she'd been living with him. Something she might think about at a later date.

Who instinctively learned the sound of one man's gait?

At the moment, however, she just wanted the man there with her. She'd done fine so far. She was a Fortune. Used to entertaining, and keeping up pleasant appearances with large groups of influential people. But the Noveltys had started asking more personal questions about Jax and she had no idea what he'd already told them, or wanted her to say.

Which was why, when he appeared in the room, she tossed a strand of hair over the shoulder of her short-sleeved T-shirt dress and unleashed a hugely pleased smile on him. And when he surprised her by leaning in for a kiss, responded a little more enthusiastically than she should have.

He covered for them. Pulling back and with a hand on her shoulder, looked over at the couple seated on what Priscilla had already adopted as her couch. Emma had a sleeping Liam cradled in her arms. Priscilla had been feeding the baby when the duo had arrived, and Emma had immediately taken over. And when Priscilla had moved to take him afterward, to lay him in his portable crib, the woman had demurred. Saying that since she hadn't seen him all week, she'd just hold him.

No asking Priscilla if she minded. After all, Emma was the boy's biological grandmother. She had genetic rights. Priscilla was just...a soon to be fake wife...who would be adopting Liam. Becoming his legal parent, regardless of the status of her marriage. Not that the Noveltys knew that.

Frank Novelty stood as Jax approached the couple. Holding out his hand, the older man said, "We're sorry for not calling first. You said we were welcome anytime, and we were out and found this little suit for Liam and wanted to drop it by." The man picked up the box they'd had Priscilla open.

Jax barely glanced at the tiniest pair of dress pants Priscilla had ever seen, the shirt and vest and bow tie. She'd oohed and ahhed over every piece. Overkill?

"I told you you're welcome anytime," Jax said, sounding...comfortable. Relaxed.

Which rubbed off on Priscilla some. A new fake fiancée meeting the ex-in-laws for the first time wasn't a part she'd ever played. Witnessed. Or imagined in her wildest dreams she'd ever be called upon to play.

"Although," he continued, walking over to Emma and laying a hand lightly against his son's cheek, "a call first would assure you a proper reception and ample time with this little guy." The reprimand was so gentle, even Priscilla wasn't certain it had been intended as one. "Or maybe we could set up a recurring schedule, that we could all plan around, for you to have your time with him." He offered something Priscilla had actually suggested to him at dinner the night before. And then came over to sit next to her on the love seat she was occupying.

Putting an arm lightly around her, he glanced out the window, and then at her, a bit of grin on his face and a knowing look in his eye.

The next fifteen minutes were a blur to Priscilla,

mostly filled with her firmly reminded affirmation that she was in control. Knew who she was. And was not willing to even consider changing the status quo. She answered when directly spoken to. Was pleasant and sociable. She could pull that off in her sleep.

Then, suddenly, the air in the room changed. She wasn't imagining it. Expressions on faces had grown melancholy. And Emma said, "It's obvious to us how doting you are, Priscilla, with this grandson of ours, and I—" the woman teared up "—I have to thank you for that from the depths of my soul. Knowing that he's being loved and watched over by your kind and giving heart…you have no idea what a blessing that is. I can relax now."

Swallowing with difficulty, Priscilla nodded, and then, looking at Liam, said, "I love him. I have from the first time I saw him. It's like he was sent to me, or I to him." Too much.

The truth. But not one she'd intended to share.

"And you two." Frank stood, held out a hand to Jax again. "It's clear that you two are really in love. Not so much from what you tried to show us, but from what you didn't. That shines through."

Priscilla smiled up at Jax as he stood to shake the older man's hand. She was putting on a show even as they'd just been called out for having done so. Because they'd been so good at it, the Noveltys had fallen for it even while they'd been on the watch for subterfuge. Fake love.

Growing bolder, she stood next to her fiancé. As Emma approached, handing over a sleeping Liam to her, she took the baby gently, focusing on his tiny puckered little lip as she cuddled him up against her.

But, good manners dictated that she had to look up

to say goodbye. She did so, to see Liam's grandmother sliding an arm around Frank's waist as he lifted his arm around her shoulders, squeezing her to him. The man seemed to swallow. He took a second to speak, at any rate, and then said, "We are grieving our daughter beyond imagination," he said, glancing at Emma who teared up. "But…" He stole another glance at his wife, who nodded, and then said, "We want what's best for Liam, and it's clear to us that that's Priscilla. We want you to know that we welcome you into the family, into Liam's life."

She was saved from reaching out to them by the baby in her arms, but she smiled, exuding the warmth that she gave to patients at the hospital, to children who were looking to her for safety as they met with a parent they didn't completely trust. Doing what she was best at. Helping others feel better.

Then, as Jax saw the couple out, she slowly climbed the massive staircase, put Liam in his crib and blinked at the tears that were filling her eyes. Refusing to allow them to fall.

Life might not be pain free, but as long as she was in control, she knew that she could handle whatever fate brought her way.

Closing the heavy front door of his family mansion behind him, Jax stood with the elation coursing through him, for the couple of seconds it took for the feeling to dissipate. Glancing at the stairs, he frowned. Priscilla's departure to put Liam in his crib had seemed appropriate.

Her not coming back down, not as much so.

She'd kept her word to him, and had done a stellar job in convincing the Noveltys that their marriage was the right answer for Liam. De-escalating any hint of a threat against Jax maintaining custody of his son. But she wasn't down there celebrating the victory with him.

Or even present to engage in any post-op debriefing.

Standing in the hallway, looking up the grand staircase, he texted her. Everything okay?

And quickly turned down his volume when the rock song started to blare almost immediately. Yes. He's squirming a bit. I'm hanging out to see if wakes up.

Staring up at the entrance to their wing of the house, he frowned. Her explanation was feasible. Given that Liam had been passed around between all of them during the visit, it was believable. And if there was a chance the baby would settle back down, there had to be minimal movement, and no sound in the nursery.

So, pocketing his phone, he went back out to work. Grabbed a sandwich from the bunkhouse kitchen at lunchtime, eating with a couple of ranch hands who lived on the property. And though he texted often, and responded when Priscilla sent him a text of Liam in his swing awake, he didn't show up at the house again until he was on baby duty.

And while he was tempted to take dinner into his office downstairs, his gut told him that it would be a wrong move. He showed up in the dining room, and saw Priscilla sitting at the table in the same flattering dress she'd had on that morning. Two place settings were set—a half-empty glass of wine at hers—and she was reading a book.

Waiting for him.

Relief flooded him. Ridiculous, uncalled-for, but there it was. He accepted the change from the knot of tension that had been growing inside him. And acknowledged that the moment he'd become a father, his life had irrevocably changed.

But that didn't mean he couldn't take charge of parts of it.

When Priscilla put down her book and moved to stand, he held out a hand. "You stay put," he told her. "I'll bring dinner in."

He'd been serving himself for the past month, he knew the ropes. And owed her far more than merely supper wait service.

Problem was, bringing her food in was the only thing he could think of to do for her.

Clearly she'd been upset by the Noveltys impromptu visit. He didn't blame her. A bit. In her shoes, he'd likely have been pissed as hell.

But she hadn't seemed angry.

He just didn't know what she *had* seemed. Had spent the day trying not think about it. While he kept running the morning over and over in his mind.

Sasha had made lasagna, and Jax stayed in the kitchen while he reheated the still warm pasta and dished up the salads that went with it. There was bread, too. He rarely ate the stuff at dinner, but had noticed that Priscilla had had bread during all three of the dinners they'd shared.

They were only eating their fourth dinner together. He could hardly wrap his mind around that fact when it hit him. He was trusting her with his son's life, sharing parenthood, and had only sat down to eat four meals with the woman?

Sometimes you just know. Something Christa had said to him when she'd told him she'd known he was going to break up with her. Right after admitting that she hadn't been in love with him, either.

And Priscilla had said something similar when she'd told her uncle and brothers about their marriage. *When you know, you know.*

He'd accepted the words from his first wife. Wanted to believe they applied to his current situation. Except that he didn't know what it was he knew.

That he could trust Priscilla to be a good mother to his son, yeah. He just knew that.

And it ended there.

Other than… Jax had to keep her happy, or risk losing her.

No, maybe not that. She'd signed on to be Liam's mother. She wasn't going to ditch the baby.

Wearing the same oven mitts Priscilla had worn the night she'd served them dinner, Jax held two full plates as he pushed through the swinging door into the dining room.

To see Priscilla's chair empty.

His heart sank. He was debating whether or not to carry the plates back into the kitchen, when she appeared with a wide awake Liam in her arms. He'd just put the baby to sleep.

"Something woke him," she said, nodding toward the monitor receiver he'd set on the table when he'd come down.

Jax set the plates down, reaching for his son, and she shook her head. "You eat, I'll hold him." He hesitated, watching her for some kind of sign of what she really wanted to do, expected of him. But when she sat, holding Liam on her left side and picked up her fork, he sat as well.

He'd eaten with the baby in his arms. Once. Had chosen to go hungry until he got Liam to sleep after that. And sat there, taking garishly large bites, trying to empty his plate as proficiently as possible so that he could relieve her.

And then started to grow uncomfortable with the silence in the room. Other than forks scraping plates, wineglasses being picked up and set down, there was very little other sound. Not even Liam had opinions or desires to express. The baby's head lay against Pricilla's breast, his eyes growing heavier and heavier.

At which point, Jax let himself off the hook conversationally. He didn't want his voice to disturb Liam's dropping off process.

His mistake was glancing at Priscilla. And catching her staring at him. He told himself to look away. But didn't.

Her gaze seemed to be roiling with emotion. Needing something from him. If he'd known what it was, he'd have given it to her.

And with Liam drifting off, he couldn't ask.

But at dinner's end, with the baby finally asleep, Jax made quick work of clearing away the dishes and then followed Priscilla upstairs.

With one fact presenting itself firmly. Over and over.

They *had* to talk.

Chapter Twelve

She had to protect her heart. Pacing in her room, Priscilla heard the words in her head like a chant. Had been listening to some form of them for hours and hours. Ever since the Noveltys had visited that morning.

She'd reached out to Jax, and he'd come galloping to her side. Seeing him walk into that room…nothing had felt more deeply, personally real to her. When he'd kissed her, sat down beside her, she'd found a sense of familiarity that wouldn't fade away.

How could she be familiar with something she'd never had?

Priscilla had made it through dinner. Could keep up appearances a good long time, apparently, years even. But was that what she wanted? Or even the healthy and best choice?

She'd made promises. Keeping them mattered.

But Emma and Frank—it was like she'd physically felt the strength they were drawing from each other in their grief. And in their ability to look forward for Liam, too. Alone, they might have fallen under the weight of their loss.

Together, they were moving into the future. A glance, a quiet touch of a hand on a thigh, a tremor from one when the other was speaking…they'd all reached her. As though someone had been in the room, armed, and with Priscilla firmly in sight, shooting her. Only her.

With impressions, things she should know, things she *did* know.

It was like her parents had been in that room that morning. Showing her what she'd once known. What she'd walled off, slowly, one year at a time, until there was nothing left but a kind compassionate volunteer.

The garden room had held them all, Jax and his son, the focal point—that which had brought them all to that place and time. And yet, there'd been a set of loving parents, grieving their daughter, and an orphaned daughter grieving her loving parents—both with something to give to the other that had nothing to do with the father and son.

But, in Priscilla's case, a whole lot to do with Jax.

She had feelings for him. Just a fact. And once acknowledged, she couldn't escape their existence. Just as she hadn't been able to stop the pain from hitting her hard when her parents had been killed. She could only take control of what was, and make choices from there.

She'd reached the same point every time she'd traveled the same mental road that day. A brick wall between her and whatever choice she made next.

Finding her journal that week had been no mistake. Just like that morning's events in the garden room, or overhearing Jax and the Noveltys the previous Monday. The way Liam had had a place in her heart the first time she'd seen him. Even the old photos, reminders of what she'd once instinctively known. And she and Jax having sex. It had all come together at once, ingredients in the recipe she'd found in the journal. Her dream life.

She wanted it.

She wanted *Jax*. But in order for the life to work, he needed to want her equally—like Frank did Emma, and her father had her mother. And like her brother Roth and Antonia.

Had that been the catalyst that first cracked Priscilla's shell? Seeing her brother in a relationship like their parents had shared? She'd felt joy for them.

She'd felt.

And hadn't stopped feeling since. Little by little. More and more.

The ice maiden thawing.

Was that why Linc had ditched her so carelessly earlier in the summer? Had he asked her out, remembering the warm, kindhearted girl she'd once been, and had ended up on a date with someone frozen inside?

Had he needed her, and she hadn't been there for him?

Dropping onto the small couch in a room easily as large as her suite at home in Dallas, Priscilla told herself to calm down. To think.

She had a wonderful place to live—three of them actually if she included Dallas and her mini mansion on the river right there in Emerald Ridge. She was intelligent enough, had talents and enough money to help change the world.

She had her health.

And could shape her future to be as bright and shining as she wanted it.

She was going to be just fine.

Because…

She was in control. And the choices were hers to make.

Only problem was, she had feelings for two men. Who

were thirty-one years apart in age. One a baby. One all grown-up man.

One who needed the love she had to pour all over him.

And one who never would.

The choice could be simple. Completely clear. If she could just choose one of them.

Unfortunately, that wasn't an option.

The Wellington men came as a pair.

Her door was shut. Turned out both of them were. The one leading in from the hallway, and the new one he'd had put in between her room and the nursery.

Taking the closed door as a message to him, Jax went in to shower off the day's grime. He made sure the water was icy cold before he made it out of the stall. Turned out, he couldn't even get naked alone without getting a hard-on for the woman who'd joined his space.

They had to talk.

Not just about the sex.

He just had to know what was concerning Priscilla. How did he hope to get things right if he had no clue what he was doing wrong? After all, you didn't go to the feed store to buy steaks for dinner. Or the grocery for a new feeding trough.

Not that Jax ever went to either. He had people who did his shopping for him. Except personal items and…what the hell…who cared about shopping?

What he needed he couldn't buy. A chance to help fix things before Priscilla changed her mind and left. He didn't want to wake up for his morning baby shift to find an engagement ring sitting on a deserted night table.

He had to know what was bothering Priscilla.

And there was only one way to find out.

In shorts and a T-shirt, he opened his bedroom door and plodded barefoot down the hallway to hers. Lifting his fist to knock, he held it there, inches from the door, allowing doubt to cloud his purpose for a few seconds, and then shaking his head, knocked softly.

He'd have called out, but didn't want to wake the baby.

Perhaps for the same reason, she didn't issue a "come in." Seconds passed and the door opened. She was still in the clothes she'd had on all day. As though she might not be done going out for the night?

The figure hugging, stretchy soft fabric was enough to tempt any guy who went for beautiful women. In Jax's home, wearing his ring, with his shower stint so recent, the woman practically knocked him to his knees. Taking a deep, calming breath, thankful for the baggy shorts with lots of pockets giving him depth behind which certain things could hide, he asked, "Can I come in?"

Stepping aside, she pulled the door open farther, and walked slowly toward an armchair in the sitting room part of her suite. Leaving only the small couch for him.

Beggars couldn't be choosy. And he most definitely was at the point of begging if need be.

Priscilla smiled at him, throwing him off balance before he could even get started finding out if indeed he'd reached that point. "What's up?" she asked. "After the long hours you put in today, you should be getting rest while you can." The concern in her tone hit him first. There was no mistaking the genuine note in her voice, nor the look in those hazel eyes turned on him.

How could it be possible that a guy felt cared about just

from a tone and a look? They couldn't, could they? Lord knew, they never had before.

The past few months were just getting to him was all. Liam's birth. Christa's death. The custody threat.

And Priscilla. The angel who'd appeared to answer his prayers. Of course he'd sense comfort coming from her. Who wouldn't when facing the one who'd rescued you?

"Honesty. Which leads to trust," he said, falling back on what he knew for sure. The promise they'd made.

Frowning, she asked, "You've been dishonest with me?" Her voice had sharpened some. He was certain about that one.

"No," he replied, sitting forward, his forearms resting on his thighs, his hands clasped. "And before you ask, I'm not accusing you of being so with me, either. I'm here because you've acted differently today, from your absence this morning, and then tonight, turning in without saying good night. I don't know why. And apparently I need to know as I'm wasting far too much brain matter on trying to figure out whether or not I've done something wrong, or have somehow offended you, or missed some nuance to which I should have spoken." Once the words started coming, he found relief in their utterance, and so added the last part. "The visit with the Noveltys today...them showing up invited...couldn't have been easy and you have a right to be upset about that and to voice those feelings."

Truth was, he'd been upset. "I know I was not happy about it," he said into her obvious silence. "I'd hoped to have a conversation with you where we commiserated with each other over the encounter. And maybe discussed how to handle similar situations in the future."

There. That was all he had. Feeling better just getting

152 FORTUNE'S FAKE MARRIAGE PLAN

it out, Jax sat back, relaxing some, as he waited for her to chime in with her share of honesty.

Many seconds passed, during which Priscilla had her gaze turned toward him, but he couldn't seem to connect with it. As though she wasn't really focusing. He was almost afraid to hear what she was going to say when she took a breath and started to speak. "I was uncomfortable with Frank and Emma being in your home without your knowledge," she admitted.

He nodded. *Yes. That. Exactly.* What he needed. Wanted. Them talking, not just wondering what the other was thinking.

"Once you were here, I think it went well," she said then. "Exactly as I imagine you'd have wanted, given that they gave you their full approval of the engagement, and seemed amenable to a visitation plan."

Well, yes, but... "I was more wondering how you were feeling, Priscilla," he said, kind of uncomfortable hearing the words coming out of his mouth. He'd never been much of one for any emotional discussion. Unless it was about how much his son owned him.

"Like I said, I was ill at ease at first, but once you were part of the conversation, it was all good."

It was good. Not *she* was good.

"I feel like I'm talking to a wall." He cringed inside as he heard his own words. He was babbling like an insecure school kid.

And he'd never been that. Not even as a preschooler.

Priscilla's gaze sharpened on him. Finally. He was getting somewhere.

"I expected you to knock on my door last night."

Oh. Ahhhh. He got instantly hard.

"I didn't want you to think that I was expecting sex just because we'd had it once. Men have a reputation for wanting it all the time," he added inanely.

"A well-deserved one for some men," she said, her chin a little high. But he saw the grin teasing the corners of her lips and the night's freneticism evaporated.

"Agreed." And then, "So I'm not at risk of waking up in the morning to a Dear John letter on the dining room table with your ring on top?"

Rolling her eyes, Priscilla shook her head. "You really think that's my way?"

"Logically, no. But…we're treading unchartered waters here and…" And he didn't know what. Shrugging, Jax left the words hanging.

Priscilla stood, seeming to signal an end to the conversation as she said, "You did the right thing, coming to talk about it. I can assure you, I have no intention of leaving any kind of a letter, ever. Nor am I on the verge of taking off my engagement ring. Like you, I'm aware of things unforeseen ahead of us, and am preferring to wade rather than swim, while I feel my way."

Standing, he grinned at her, then said, "Perhaps if I did a little more wading, rather than diving in before I know anything about the bottom of the pool…"

She'd moved toward her door. Clearly getting rid of him. Probably with the intent of saving them both from his uncharacteristic nonsensical agitation. A good move.

Following her, he was suddenly overeager to get out of there. To return to his own room, find something brainless to stream, and get what rest he could before Liam was demanding his attention.

He was already contemplating possible streaming

choices and didn't notice quickly enough when Priscilla suddenly stopped in front of him. He barreled right into her. Grabbing her arms instinctively, holding her upright, he glanced down to see a hint of darkness in her eyes as she looked up at him.

"Have you been contemplating leaving *me* a Dear John letter?" she asked him. "Are you getting cold feet? Because if you are, then we definitely do need to talk…".

Her lips were parted as her words trailed off. She was still gazing right into his eyes, but her expression had changed. And her body pressed ever so lightly against his.

She'd become aware of his hard-on.

And suddenly he could think of little else. "No…cold… feet." He got the words out, slowly, as he lowered his head and kissed her.

Like the hungry man he was. Wholly. Completely. Full on and ready.

The response from Priscilla's lips ignited him. Wiping out all reality but her. Without breaking the kiss, he backed her toward her bed, fell down to it with her, cushioning them as best he could, and then rolled over on top of her.

He didn't ask. He just did. Whatever their bodies drove him to do.

Didn't think, just felt. His own desire, but hers too. All over him. Kissing, touching, driving him to the brink again and again.

It wasn't that he was letting her lead, it was that they were on the path together, running, hand in hand, toward a precipice that promised fulfillment beyond their wildest dreams. But they had to get there. Together.

When he was certain he could hold on no more, she

grabbed a condom from her bedside drawer, sheathed and straddled him, sliding herself down on top of him. He fondled her, she arched back, tightening around him and they reached their goal as one. Exploding in ecstasy.

When it was over, she fell sideways to the bed, leaving him to make a quick trip to her bathroom. His heart was still pounding, blood thrumming through his veins, when he stepped back into the bedroom, thinking about another go. However, he stopped short when he saw Priscilla had pulled down the covers and was lying, still gloriously naked, on the bottom sheet, eyes shut.

Nothing about her spoke "second time." Yet she still called to him. Figuring he'd just lie down next to her for a moment, he lowered himself to the bed. Then closed his eyes too, just to rest them for a second, to let himself come down from the extraordinary physical experience he'd just been through.

And the next thing he knew, Liam's cry woke him.

Confused in that first instant, he glanced toward the only light he could see, a clock not far from him. And then sat straight up. Gut heavy with the magnitude of his mistake.

Three hours had passed and he was still in Priscilla's bed.

Priscilla felt Jax leave the bed. But all cuddled up, feeling warm and content, she went back to sleep, so she'd be ready when her own turn came to tend to the baby they shared. Jax would open her door when he put the baby back down after his next feeding.

Except, he didn't. It was almost four in the morning before she heard the baby cry, and threw off the covers, heart pounding with alarm. Had she slept through an entire feeding?

Pulling on her robe as she rushed into the room, she flipped on the overhead light, noticed Jax's door still open, and almost barreled into him as he came racing toward her. She reached the crib first. Picked up the baby, her eyes taking in every inch of his body, noting the still-dry sleeper, and the very wet face.

Not speaking—she wouldn't be heard above the angry screams—she changed Liam, noting that his diaper was heavier than any other had been. By far. And then, with his sleeper secured back in place, lifted him and turned, to see Jax handing her a warmed bottle.

"I'm so sorry," she told him, the second the infant's lips took the nipple and miraculous silence fell.

Heading to the rocker, she sat and heard, "Sorry for what?"

"Missing my turn. Why didn't you wake me?"

Frowning, Jax looked at her. "I thought I'd missed mine," he told her. And then, his expression clearing, he stared at her. "He slept through it!" he said.

Just as she stated, "He almost slept all night!"

They both fell silent, grinning at each other as though they were somehow responsible for nature's way with growing babies.

And in the moment, Priscilla felt certain that nature at work was just a part of her and Jax's relationship. They were two people who'd thought they'd be living life alone who were simply meant to be.

"By the way, something I need to discuss with you," he said, leaning back against the wall as he watched her feeding his son.

Nodding, she took pleasure in watching him there, comfortable in only the briefs he'd obviously been sleeping in, and feeling better than she had in a long time, murmured, "What's up?"

"What happened in there earlier." He waved a hand toward her room, and her belly took a pleasurable leap. "It can't happen anymore."

Wait. What? Frowning, figuring she was misunderstanding his shorthand type conversation, she asked thickly, "What do you mean?"

"The sex. It got control of us. Drove us to do things without thinking. Without consideration to the ramifications…"

Confused, she shook her head and said, "We used a condom. After the first time, I put them specifically in the drawer for that purpose. That *was* thinking. And considering consequences." He couldn't have missed that part. Even if he'd been so on fire he'd hardly noticed her putting it on him, he'd had to leave the bed to take it off.

"There are a lot of other potential consequences besides pregnancy to consider, Priscilla. Anything that makes you lose control, that makes you act without thinking, is dangerous. When feelings are out of hand, things get messy. And sometimes things are said, or done, that are later regretted. Or, or false expectations are built and people get hurt."

Everything inside Priscilla stilled as she listened to him ramble. She'd wonder at some point what part, exactly, of their lovemaking he regretted, but at that moment, all she could do was rock slowly and feed his baby.

As though sensing the change in her, Jax stood straight, his expression becoming almost pleading as he said, "For our marriage to be a success, to ensure that we retain custody of Liam without the Noveltys interfering, we have to guard against anything that could destroy our friendship or cause problems between us."

Intellectually Priscilla understood, and so she slid, pretty naturally, into the space inside her that she'd been occupying her entire adult life. The one that had forgotten childish dreams for her future. Because while she didn't see where the mind-blowing perfection of her and Jax's coming together could in any way destroy their friendship or create problems between them, the fact that he apparently did proved him right. She didn't have a problem with the sex, but he obviously did.

Which created a crack in their relationship.

And...hurt feelings. *Hers.*

Because she'd developed some for Jax. Deep and abiding ones. "I'm not sure that you can walk back sex, Jax," she told him. "I'm not even sure that it's healthy to try. I get what you're saying here, but Liam needs to be raised in a home where all parts of him can thrive. Not only the intellectual part, but the emotional being inside him, too. He learns that through the relationships around him. Most particularly us. And while he wouldn't be privy to our sex lives, obviously, he would detect a distance in us if we're sleeping in separate rooms..." No, that's *not* what she'd meant.

They'd never talked about sharing a bedroom. But apparently in some part of her psyche she'd been thinking about it. Which just once again proved Jax's point in terms of the complications sex was bringing to their relationship.

"It's just... Liam deserves parents who are willing to fight for their marriage." The word *love* had almost fallen off the tip of her tongue. But she wasn't ready to go there yet. Not even just to herself. Yes, her heart reacted strongly to Jax, but that didn't mean for sure that she was in love with him. "He will grow up more well-adjusted if he has parents who are committed to their relationship," she said, finishing her observations tepidly.

Crossing his arms, Jax frowned down at her. "I thought we *were* committed to our marriage. I know I am. Are you telling me you aren't?"

"No!" She spoke so loudly the baby jumped. And she took a deep breath, finishing softly with, "I'm fully committed. I'm just not sure that no sex is the answer."

Waving his hand, he took a step closer, then stopped. "Look at us right now, tension and disagreement between us after having just done it twice."

Yeah, she'd already—silently—acknowledged the validity of his point. But felt driven to say, "And you think us going around turned on, living with unrequited desire, is somehow going to create a more amiable atmosphere?"

When he stood there staring at her, hard, she added softly, "Liam needs parents who are willing to work on whatever problems they have, Jax, not walk on eggshells in an attempt not to have any problems. That's not life. It's not realistic."

He nodded, and she took hope, until he said, "I'm not for one second thinking there won't be issues and challenges, Priscilla," he told her. "But this here, right now, is me trying to work on a problem I'm telling you I'm having. I only know how to have casual sex. It's who I am. What I do. And I can't do that to you." He threw up his hands.

And, hearing the backhanded avowal that she meant

more to him than other women in his life had, Priscilla bowed her head.

Hiding the tears that sprang to her eyes.

Chapter Thirteen

Jax couldn't back down.

Or rather, he could—and would—if Priscilla said sex had become a breaking point for her. She knew he wanted her. He'd left zero doubt about that one.

But he didn't believe that continuing to be intimate with Priscilla was the right thing to do. The entire day before he'd been off his mark, distracted by concerns that she was distressed about something, and she had been. Because he hadn't gone to her room Friday night. He'd never given any indication that he would, and yet, she'd expected him to do so and had been upset when he hadn't.

Sex didn't just give rise to feelings of desire, but with some people, it put other emotions on high gear, too. He wasn't one of those people. Evidently, Priscilla was.

Though she'd said differently the first few times they'd spoken about it.

Seeing her bowed head, he couldn't just walk away. Had to try harder to help her understand. To explain himself.

"Christa wanted a real marriage," he told her. "Even knowing that neither of us were in love with the other, or even compatible for more than a fun night out. She'd said it would make our commitment to each other more solid. Bring us closer. Hold us together. And you are the one person who knows how that worked out."

She raised her head to meet his gaze, nodding slowly. And Jax started to breathe a bit easier.

Sex with him hadn't kept Christa out of another man's arms. It had only made her affair harder to accept.

"Our...family...is different, Priscilla. We're both coming from the same place, in terms of relationships. And we're going to work because our marriage is going to be based on things that last long past the time when sexual desire fades. We share mutual admiration, respect, and most of all, truth and trust."

Still watching him, her expression clear, she nodded once again.

And feeling as though he was fighting for his life, as well as that of his son's, he pushed on. "To keep all of that, we can't lose who we were when we decided to take this step together. We have to maintain our individualism. Our autonomy."

Sighing, Priscilla looked down at Liam, jiggling his bottle just enough to see that his lips were still holding tight, then looked back up at Jax and said, "I agree with most of that, but we're going to lose who we were, Jax. We've already moved on from those people. Every day, things happen and people are affected by them. We learn something new. Sometimes, how to roll with the punches. Or discover something about ourselves that hadn't revealed itself to us prior to that. Things maybe we weren't ready to know. Or hadn't yet matured to the point that we could see or recognize something about ourselves. It's called living life."

He heard the words. Understood them. Struggled to

read between the lines to figure out what she was really trying to tell him.

Then wondered if there *was* more there. If he was messing things up by trying too hard. Making more out of less. He'd heard his father say something like that to his mother once. He hadn't understood it at the time, any better than he was getting Priscilla in the moment.

Until she said, "I'm committed to the future we've agreed to build together," and his world righted itself. Whatever else was going on, they were okay.

"And I won't do anything that's going to jeopardize Liam's custody, or disenchant his grandparents where you and or I am concerned," she continued, making him tense all over again.

He heard the "but" coming even before she said, "But maybe we should wait on the marriage a bit, until we're more on the same page."

And while he nodded, told her he'd wait however long it took for her to be ready, and retreated to his room, Jax was no longer so certain that things were going to work out for them.

Because he was who he was and that wasn't going to change. Even if she had the gift of reinventing herself with every new day that dawned and brought her new things to learn about herself. Or a maturity that helped her see things differently. Or any of the other things she'd just said.

Breaking it down to simple language, when it came to relationships with people, he was a casual guy who, other than his son, didn't see himself giving his all to anyone. It wasn't in him to do so.

Bottom line, he just plain didn't know how to be the man she needed.

And he was beginning to think that, in the end, Priscilla wouldn't be able to settle for anything less than that.

Moreover, he would never ask her to do so.

Which left him feeling pretty much out of luck.

Unless there was an emergency on the ranch, Jax didn't work on Sundays. He'd said as much the first day Priscilla had been in his home—while going over schedules with her and Bonita, the nanny who'd been let go.

As she watched his butt retreat from their conversation that early predawn Sunday morning, Priscilla continued to rock the sleeping baby who already owned her heart. And knew she needed some space.

It had all been too much. His so romantic proposal—enacted for practical purposes—the mind-blowing sex. The marriage license followed by a celebratory family dinner, and more sex. The conversations and promises of honesty. The journal she'd found reacquainting her with the younger self she'd forgotten, but now couldn't forget. The photos her parents had taken not long before their deaths…

She could be forgiven for being unable to contain the emotions roiling up inside her.

But maybe she didn't need to be.

She wanted what her parents had had. What it appeared the Noveltys shared. What Roth had just found. The dream life she'd written about in her journal so many years before. When her parents' married life had still been shining brightly inside her.

But she couldn't just flit off into the sunset in search

of a dream. She'd made commitments. And she'd fallen in love. With a helpless, vulnerable three-month-old child who'd already become a son to her.

Staring at the door that Jax had closed quietly, but it had seemed quite firmly, behind him, Priscilla considered the possibility that she'd fallen in love with the father, too.

Fallen for a man who would never love her back.

And if she had?

Did one get over such feelings? Or merely push them inside, carry them along, for the rest of their lives? How did another man fit into that scenario in the future? How did the dream come true with her heart already planted at Wellington Ranch?

She asked the questions. Received nothing but blank space in her brain in response. But knew with Jax home that day, she shouldn't be there. She'd had Liam all to herself for a couple of days. His father deserved the same.

And she needed time on her family estate, visiting with anyone who might be home, looking through the photos that had been developed and dropped off at each of their cottages the day before, settling in with herself in the hopes of finding answers to guide the rest of her life.

It was a big ask. But if she was going to be in control of her life, she had to do the work to find her answers.

After laying Liam carefully in his crib, she didn't go back to bed. She showered. Dressed in a pair of stretchy capri pants, a crop top, blue bling wedged slip-on sandals, and grabbed her keys. She texted Jax from her car, letting him know she'd be gone for the day, but would be back in plenty of time for her evening Liam duties, and left the ranch.

Feeling, as she pulled out onto the road that would lead

into town, that she was leaving a part of her heart behind. She stopped for a caramel latte at Coffee Connection. Sat in the park to drink it while watching the sunrise. And then headed to her cottage on the river. Taking her time. Noticing the shapes of clouds, the glistening leaves as the sun shone down upon them. The lush green grass.

She didn't tell anyone she'd be home. Just drove to her house and went inside as she'd been doing all summer. And saw, first thing, the thick envelope of photos Uncle Sander had left on the table around which her entire family had been sitting such a short time before.

It seemed like months since she'd seen them. She'd traveled so far back, and then forward again in the past couple of days. It almost felt like they'd know. That she'd look different to them.

And maybe she would. Expressions, eyes, mannerisms matured as people experienced life. She'd seen it in others. In Roth, over the past month.

She'd laid out the photos, had them spread all over her large dining table, and the kitchen counters, too, and was walking around among them, taking them all in, when her cell rang. Expecting the call to be from Jax, she almost let it go.

Almost. But what if something had happened with Liam…?

The caller wasn't Jax. It was Sam James, one of the detectives working on Linc's murder case. The forensic computer expert. Someone she'd known peripherally years before. A boy who hadn't been a part of their crowd, but one of her friends had been dating him behind her parents' backs.

Calling her on a Sunday morning?

"I'm sorry to bother you so early on a Sunday morning, Priscilla, but I had an idea that led to, well, it doesn't matter what… The bottom line is, I've been up half the night and I finally got into Linc's bank accounts."

And he was calling her? Not his boss? Or Roth or Uncle Sander?

He knew she'd stepped out of her circle to go out with Linc that summer. Just as her friend had done with him.

Difference being that she'd grown up with Linc. With his mother working for their family, she'd seen him practically every day. Had eaten meals with him.

She didn't want to know what the computer guru had found. Didn't want to hear that Linc had amassed a fortune selling illegally obtained documents.

"What did you find?" she asked anyway. Because she was done blocking out the hard stuff. Hiding from herself. "He was rich, right?"

"No," Sam said, his tone almost eager sounding. "That's just it. There's only a few hundred dollars here. It's clear that he didn't sell any of the adoption records, if he even had them, because there is no money anywhere."

She was confused. Trying not to let herself hope. "That doesn't make any sense," she told him. "The whole point of him buying the records from the adoption agency worker who was dying was to sell them and make enough money to give him status."

Something she'd tried to tell him that summer that he already had. Just by being the great guy he was. But then she'd never been in his shoes, without enough money to cushion all blows.

"Yeah, it's not what any of us were expecting, but that's not why I'm calling you," he said. "I've already made some calls and cleared this with the higher-ups, and wanted to be the one to let you know…"

"Know what?" she asked.

"That the password I generated that allowed me access to Linc's bank accounts also got me into another site he'd visited recently. For online will creation. I found his—it's been legally vetted as a favor to me this morning—and I wanted you to be the first to know so you aren't blind-sided…" There was a long pause. "He left everything to you, Priscilla."

Say what? The words that Linc had bestowed all his worldly possessions to her echoed through her mind. Over and over again.

"I don't understand…" she began. She'd gone out with Linc once, and then he'd ditched her. Why would he…

"It's not much," the detective said. "The few hundred dollars I told you about, and his houseboat. Apparently, he was living on it, but I have to warn you, it's in disre-pair. At least according to the owner of the marina who has been made aware that there's a transfer of title. And we have the keys here at the police station. They were among Linc's belongings…"

Linc, who she'd thought had been repulsed by her, had left her all of his worldly possessions? Something else in her life that wasn't what it had seemed. Or…was it? Linc's treatment of her, his death, the scandal he was involved in—those weren't at all in line with what she'd known and believed about the man.

So, was the fact that he hadn't sold adoption records evidence that Linc hadn't been involved in something sordid after all?

But then, how did that explain Linc approaching Finn

Morrison, her sister Zara's ex-boyfriend, trying to sell Finn his adoption records?

Needing answers, Priscilla told the detective she'd stop by the police station that morning to pick up the keys, and then, without a word to anyone, she collected all of her photos, put them in her bag, locked up her cottage and headed out. Odd circumstances had been presenting all week long. As though her parents had had enough of her lollygagging and were pointing her toward more. No way she could ignore the strange phone call.

And while she didn't really believe that Linc's having left her his houseboat had anything to do with divine inspiration, neither could she, in good conscience, just ignore the news. She might not be able to find solutions for herself, but if she could help clear the shadow over a dead man's life, maybe she could at least find some peace.

In just a week, Priscilla had made his mansion, the place where he'd grown up, feel like a home. A real one. Where everyone inside it was connected not by law, but by awareness of each other. A conscious choice to reach out to each other. A place where expectations weren't charts by which one was judged, but rather, as road maps to happiness.

Road maps to happiness. Definitely not a Jax thought. The woman was even invading his thoughts.

He didn't like it. Not a bit. Although the contributions weren't abhorrent. Or even wrong.

But they confused him as often as not.

Jax did not like being perplexed. At least not when his own thoughts and feelings were bewildering him.

He had to get out of the house. Priscilla was everywhere. Or rather, her absence was obvious in every room he entered, except his own. And even there…he'd spent the night with her there, mentally, in his bed. And had had her in the shower, too, more than once since she'd moved in—showering away his body's response to her with frigid cold water that he'd hoped would wash his desire down the drain.

It hadn't yet.

But it wasn't the negative that was driving him out toward the bunkhouse and Rufus, the old ranch hand who'd been the closest thing Jax had noticed to being a friend to his father. Or rather, the only person he'd known his father to treat like a trusted friend.

It was the rest, the stuff he couldn't trust himself to contribute, that prompted Jax to dress his son in jeans, a red plaid shirt and the tiniest cowboy boots he'd ever seen and call Rufus—the man didn't do texts—and let him know they were coming for a visit. With Liam perched on one arm, Jax one-handedly pushed the baby's stroller along the path to the bunkhouse. And the little cabin behind it where Rufus now had his own space. The area was quiet that Sunday morning as hands either slept off the night before, or were away on their own personal pursuits during their day off.

A couple of guys holding cups of coffee tilted their cowboy hats to him as he passed. Jax let go of the stroller long enough to return the gesture, and for a second there, with his son in his arms, and walking on the land he now owned and ran, he felt tall and proud.

Priscilla might call the sensation happiness. He shook his head at the intrusive thought.

And sank back to his uneasy spirits as the woman once

again invaded his mind. He was between a rock and a hard place, as Rufus used to say. A no-win situation. He was pretty sure he could compel Priscilla to keep her word, to marry him and ensure Liam's future security there on the ranch. But how could he possibly live with himself if he knowingly let the woman sacrifice her own happiness, her personal need for a deeper adult one-on-one relationship?

But how did he possibly give her something he didn't have to give? She'd see through pretense. And dishonesty would only damage the good part of their union. The trust they'd already managed to build.

Jax hadn't planned to discuss any of his quandaries with Rufus. But as he sat on the thin padding of the man's couch, watching as Rufus, in his log rocking chair, held a sleeping Liam, he ended up spilling his guts like a little kid.

Maybe because the old man was the one he'd run to every time he'd been upset as a kid. Rufus was not only wise, but was known for keeping his own counsel. Unless a life was at stake, as it had been a couple of months before when a woman had lied about being the mother of an abandoned baby and Rufus had known that the real mother was a desperate young ranch hand right there on Wellington Ranch. More of his stepmother's evilness at work. And Rufus's testimony had led authorities to the proper mother, and helped exposed some of Courtney's illegal dealings.

Leaning forward, his elbows on his knees, he looked at the ranch hand and said, "I care about her too much to let her give up her own inherent needs," he said, finishing his Priscilla tirade on a low note.

The old man eyed him seriously. As though telling Jax

that there was more he wasn't saying. He knew the look. Was at a total loss.

"What?" he finally had to ask.

"Seems to me you're finally falling in love," the man said, as though he was talking about a cow giving birth. A natural occurrence that happened regularly, in multiple incidents a day sometimes around the ranch.

Jax rolled his eyes. "Now's not the time for pulling my leg, Old Man," he muttered. "This is me, we're talking about."

Rufus didn't even begin to crack a hint of a smile. His expression still steely as his gaze pinned Jax, he said, "You love that boy."

Jax gave one certain bob of his head. "I'd give my life for him."

"And you think love comes in flavors?" the old man asked then. "'Cause it don't. You got the capacity to love that deep, same stuff is going to pour out again if someone touches you just right. And I ain't talking about your Johnny down there, boy." Rufus said with a nod toward Jax's fly. "Just making that one clear."

Jax had expected more from Rufus. A like mind that made sure he stayed on course. "I'm my father's son," he said, his disappointment in the guy's response evident in his tone. The first time he sought out the old ranch hand as an adult and he got…tiddlywinks.

"And your mother's and God's, too," Rufus came back, still aiming bullets with his eyes straight at Jax as he continued. "Some people's born without the ability to feel real emotion, but that ain't you. Wasn't your father, either. He just got eaten up by the wrong feelings. The ones in his pants. But he loved you and your sister. And in his own way, he loved your mother, too. Drank himself into a stupor sitting right there where you are the night she died."

Everything within Jax stilled. He stared at Rufus, wondering, for a second, if the old man was having memory issues. The second the doctor had pronounced Jax's mother dead, his father and left the sick room set up in the nonfamily wing of the mansion, stormed out the front door and gone into town. For the night. Just as Jax had known him to do when he'd spent the night in another woman's bed. Information Jax had been privy to from puberty. And something forever hidden from Annelise. Whether or not Jax's mom had known he'd never had the courage to try to find out.

He must have spoken at least some of what he was reliving aloud as Rufus said, "He picked up a couple of fifths in town, came straight here and drank until he passed out. That night and half a dozen afterward, too."

Jax, who'd been handling Annelise's grief as best he could on his own, had figured his father for hooking up with Courtney during that week. They'd married so soon after his mother's death…

Jax couldn't wrap his mind around what he was hearing. "You sure about this?" he had to ask.

Rufus sighed, glanced down at Liam, and said, "You remember him having his hand wrapped up? Said he hurt it tussling with a horse in the barn?"

Jax remembered. There'd been no evidence of anything gone astray in any barns on the property. He'd checked them out himself. His father hadn't been able to name which horse. Jax had been hell bent on putting the crazed animal down before he hurt himself or someone else.

"Go look under that calendar hanging there," Rufus said, nodding to the wall to his right.

Jax rose slowly, glancing from the ranch hand to the calendar. Then approached cautiously, not sure he wanted to go any farther, but in the end, had to do as he'd been bid. He'd come to Rufus seeking answers. Or, more realistically, closure on what he'd believed could be his own miracle. Pulling down the calendar, he saw a fist-sized dent in the wall. With what looked to be dried blood in the middle of it.

"He did that the night she died," Rufus said gruffly. "Hated himself for cheating on her. And hoped to God she hadn't known."

"Why didn't you get this fixed?" Jax spat out, frowning. "I'll have someone over here first thing in the morning and—"

"No." Rufus just sat there rocking. Shaking his head. "It's the night your father met his heart, Jax. The reminder's important, right now, so's you can see it. And maybe, when this little guy grows up, he'll need to see it, too. You Wellington men are hard sons of—" Cutting himself off midstream, Rufus looked down at the baby he held. And shrugged.

Jax wanted to believe the old man. Wanted to think that a fist print in a wall could really change him.

But he knew better than to believe in fairy tales.

Chapter Fourteen

The houseboat was indeed in disrepair. To put it mildly. Paint was peeling. Parts of the galley floor were loosening and curling up. The bathroom sink drain had rust rimming it, and the toilet hadn't been cleaned in far too long.

The shower looked okay.

Walking slowly through the place, she hated that it had been Linc's home. She'd had no idea when she'd gone out with him that summer that he'd been in such dire straits. While his pride wouldn't have let him take a handout—nor would she have offered one—she could easily have found ways to share her wealth with him. She'd have hired him to remodel her cottage if it came to that.

And let him stay there while he did so. Uncle Sander would have welcomed her at the big house. There was certainly enough space there as, when her parents had been alive, they'd lived there with all four kids all summer long.

Pulling open the refrigerator door, she shoved it closed quickly before she gagged. The electricity was still on, but something inside that small appliance was badly spoiled.

The stove had a burner pan missing while the oven appeared as though it had never been cleaned. And the small table had a corner cracked off, leaving raw wood exposed.

She found a newer set of plastic dishes in a cupboard,

thankfully all clean, with some matching plastic drinking glasses. And the silverware was also untarnished and lined neatly in a drawer.

Canned goods in the other cupboard hadn't yet expired. She was surprised to see how many of them contained beans. As a kid, Linc hadn't liked vegetables much. She remembered him being told to eat his veggies all the time. And that he'd had to go without dessert for not having done so.

The small built-in sofa had a tear in the leather covering it. And paper covering the wall behind it was peeling. By the looks of things, water had come in from the porthole window above it. Because it had been left open, or had a leak, she had no idea.

A television remote lay on the only chair. She clicked and the small screen came on. Showing her nothing but old-fashioned snow. There was no stereo equipment, no router, modem or streaming device that she could see. More likely, Linc streamed from his phone. She knew he'd had one of those. He'd pulled it out to take a call the night they'd been out together.

She stopped to look at the couple of books lined up in what was probably at one time intended to be a small china cupboard, judging by the glass door. Which had a diagonal crack running from a top corner across to the opposite bottom one. Opening the door gingerly, she pulled out the books. Smiled when saw *Moby Dick*. She'd grumbled one summer about having to read the book for her advanced literature class, and Linc had told her she was missing the whole point of the story. He'd read the book twice, and hadn't even had to. He'd just wanted to.

Tearing up, she put the book back where she'd found it.

Not really absorbing yet that it now belonged to her. She'd grown up thinking of Linc as part of their family. Being the son of their adored live-in housekeeper, he'd certainly been a part of the household. But in his teen years, Linc had started to hold himself apart from Priscilla and her siblings. She'd never been sure why.

And found it harder to accept that he'd left everything he'd owned to her.

As though to make up for the way he'd cut her off that summer? Saying he'd call and then not doing so?

She'd taken it personally. Thinking that she'd turned him off somehow. Not a big surprise in light of the fact that her entire dating life had kind of been that way. Her never finding a genuine connection with any of the men she'd dated.

Until Jax.

Thoughts of the man sent a wave of sorrow washing over her. Along with a warmth she couldn't deny. She'd once heard one of her friends say, "when it's right, it's right" but could "it" be right after only a week of actually spending time together?

She and Jax didn't want the same kind of relationship. She'd thought they were on the same page when they'd first negotiated the terms of their arrangement. But it wasn't *his* fault that she'd suddenly changed course on him.

Could it be right and wrong at the same time?

Moving back to the bedroom—funny how thoughts of Jax always ended up leading her to bed—Priscilla teared up again as she opened a small sliding closet door and saw Linc's clothes lined up in perfect order. Hangers all the same, quarter inch apart. She soon saw where some of his money had gone. Not thousands, but easily hundreds of dollars. Everything was designer made. From the tuxedo to the jeans. Same with the shoes. The man might not have made the fortune he'd sworn as a teen that he was going to make, but he'd certainly dressed as though he had. The thought made her sad all over again, and she closed the closet. Figuring she'd donate the clothes to a secondhand shop in Dallas that she knew of.

Rounding the bed, she almost fell as she leaned on it, felt it give and lost her balance. She righted herself, then pulled up on the mattress, to see what had made it go down in the first place. And jumped back as the whole thing started to rise.

Pushing farther, she saw the springs underneath the plywood upon which the mattress was mounted, and then lifted the thing all the way up.

Instead of a box spring under the mattress, as she'd expected to find there, she was looking into a relatively new—based on the hinges—secret storage space under the bed.

And staring at a slew of files. Old ones based on the tattered edges.

Heading out to the kitchen, Priscilla grabbed a couple of cleaning gloves she'd noticed—with a dose of irony—under the sink and yanked them on. Every step back to the bedroom filled her heart with dread. She'd seen the label on the top file.

Texas Royale Private Adoption Agency.

An agency that had been found to have "sold" babies to very wealthy families.

She had to be looking at the files that Linc had purchased illegally with the intent to blackmail their rightful owners into buying them or have them exposed.

Climbing under the raised bed, Priscilla sat on the floor and, with gloved hands, picked up the files one by one. Looking at the names on them. Some folders in the pile had names written on the outside of them, as though Linc did research into the adoptees family members or something. She didn't know what they meant.

But she counted and knew that she had twenty-seven different babies represented right there on her lap and the floor around her.

Oddly enough, Finn Morrison was not among the names on the files. Pulling her phone out of the waistband of her pants, she hit redial for the detective she'd spoken to earlier. Told him what she'd found. And then just sat there. Too sad to cry.

Trying to make sense of lives gone so far askew.

People who were raised as biological heirs who weren't even lawfully adopted. Legally, probably, but not through proper channels.

And as she thumbed through folders, thinking of the twenty-seven babies who'd been given up by their mothers, something else occurred to her.

Picking up her phone from the floor where she'd dropped it, she called Zara. Her sister had been badly hurt by Finn when they were younger, but Priscilla knew that Zara still had an interest in knowing why the man had come forward as he had after Linc's death.

"Hey," she said softly when her sister picked up. "I was just thinking about Linc, about Finn's claim that he'd tried to sell him his adoption papers…"

"Yeah." Zara tried to sound nonchalant, but Priscilla

heard through the practiced tone to the young woman she'd watched sobbing with a broken heart.

"Something doesn't track," Priscilla said then, not sure why it mattered, but glad to have some kind of clarity of thought. "The Texas Royale Adoption Agency sold babies to wealthy families. But the Morrisons were working class." It had been part of the reason Finn had broken things off with Zara. They were in different leagues. "How did they afford the agency's exorbitant fees?"

She was looking at the amounts. Right there in front of her.

And it didn't make sense.

Just like the rest of her life.

"I don't know." Zara's tone echoed the sadness reverberating through Priscilla as she continued to study the files. Horrified and yet mesmerized by the evidence.

She chatted with her sister for a couple of more minutes. Mostly answering questions about Jax, asserting—with truth—that she really did have feelings for the man, and no, she wasn't just taking her need to help people to a whole new level. And then, feeling guilty, but not enough to prevent her from doing so, she told her sister that duty called and she had to go.

Without telling Zara where she was. Or why.

The police would contact Roth. Or Uncle Sander. Probably not on a Sunday morning, but by the next day, for sure. They'd all know about Priscilla's bizarre little inheritance soon enough.

But for the moment, she didn't want them there. Hovering over her. Putting their thoughts in her head.

She needed time to herself. To gain at least a semblance

of control. To know her own mind before others told her what to think.

Most of all, she wanted to cry. About Linc. The fact that he really had had the records. And that they likely got him killed. Though since he hadn't sold any of them, why anyone would want him dead, she didn't get.

Just as she didn't fully understand why she was still just sitting there. Her body almost felt like deadweight. Her world consisting only of her and the illegally gained files.

Why had Linc left her the houseboat? Had he known his life was in danger? Wanted her to find the files? Or had he thought she never would?

The whole thing was unnerving her to the point of motionlessness.

Or maybe it had just been the last straw for a heart newly opened and raw. Because while her life was changing dramatically, once again, her heart was with Liam and Jax.

She had to try to figure out how she lived with the man without any kind of personal relationship between them—other than friendship.

They'd be good friends.

The thought brought a surge of doubt to her shivering insides. Could she be happy with him as a close friend for the rest of their lives? Her best friend?

She'd never really had one of those, either.

What a mess everything was. She finally found a man who fit the dream life she'd given up on and he didn't want to live her dream. And the whole thing with Linc… she just couldn't make sense of it all. Dejected, she riffled through another couple of files, figuring the police would be there shortly to take possession of them. Hoping they solved the case quickly.

But finding no similar emotion when her thoughts turned once again to Jax.

Because life had taught her young about the absence of hope, too.

Sometimes there just wasn't a happy ending.

Lunchtime had come and gone. Two naptimes had happened. Jax strolled Liam through the barns, held the baby boy up to Samson—the horse he'd already picked for his son to learn on—and talked to him about the beef cattle operation that Liam would someday inherit.

While the baby slept, he took care of ranch business that had piled up in his office during the week. Had a preseason football game on in the background.

And he thought of Priscilla every step of the way. All day. Priscilla. How could someone who'd only been in his home for a week, have so completely filled it with her presence? Her positive attitude had permeated the place. But without her in it, the air felt stale.

Why hadn't she called? Or at least texted to check on Liam? Was she letting go of them?

He hadn't texted her, to report in, as she did with him when he was in the field all day. Because if she wanted out, he had to let her walk away.

But what if she didn't want out and he was *cutting* her out?

Standing in the garden room with a freshly changed and fed Liam resting against his chest, Jax stopped short before putting the still conscious baby in his swing. Until Priscilla had joined the household, Jax had never visited the garden room. Sasha had brought the swing in. She spent time there. Jax hadn't used the swing since.

Priscilla had left open the door between her room and the nursery. Her things had all been there. No trunk in sight. After almost a week of full time Liam and Jax, she'd taken a day to herself, probably to visit her family and have some quiet time in her cottage, and he was acting as though she'd left them permanently.

The fact that she should do so existed.

And then what, he'd pretend like he'd never known her? Just cut her off because they needed different things?

They didn't have to be engaged or married to be friends. She loved his son. That mattered.

Holding Liam with one arm, he pulled his phone out of his shirt pocket and dialed. Was pleasantly surprised when he heard her pick up after half a ring. "Jax?"

Just the one word and his gut clenched. "What's wrong?"

"Nothing." She didn't sound frightened, which calmed him some.

She could be with someone. "Is this a bad time?"

"No. Just… I got a call from the police this morning. Linc left everything he had to me, Jax. It wasn't much, just this sad old houseboat he was living on, but I found the adoption records. You know, the ones he'd supposedly bought from the former agency employee and that they thought were likely involved in his murder? He didn't sell them, Jax. They're all right here, except for Finn's…"

Grabbing his keys, he headed for the door. "Where are you?"

"At the marina. Linc's houseboat…"

"Are you alone?"

"Yeah, the police are coming to get the records…"

"I'm on my way."

He didn't analyze, or even question the choice. And when, as he strapped Liam in his car seat in the back of his truck, he had a second's hesitation, he shook his head and worked faster. Priscilla was struggling and she hadn't called her family.

But she'd answered his call on the first ring. Sounding like she needed a friend.

And no matter what kind of future they had together, he was going to be her friend. That day and always.

Done deal.

The police had been and gone. Pulling the mattress back down, Priscilla straightened the bedding on top of it and turned a circle in the small space, engulfed in uncharacteristic listlessness.

Linc's life had to have amounted to more than just a decrepit boat and a few hundred dollars. There *had* to be more.

He'd wanted more, she knew that. Had planned to make millions. Sad that the need for money had driven him into illegal channels.

And that he had no family to mourn him except Priscilla and her siblings—all of whom he'd shunned in later years. And for what?

Life was too short, the people in it too precious, to waste a day of blessing them. That's what she'd grown up knowing. Her life mattered as long as she was helping others. As her parents had done. As they'd shown her by example every day of her growing up.

"You here?" Jax's voice calling out to her, in just that second, was like a beacon in the darkness.

"Yes!" she called back. Hurrying to the front of the boat, her gaze meeting his briefly and then settling on the car seat carrier he held. Liam.

A new, sweet precious life yet to be taught, to be molded, to be loved. "I'll take him," she said, reaching for the carrier. Jax didn't hesitate even a second before handing his son over to her, and then climbed aboard the sorrowful vessel himself. She stayed with Liam while he took a quick look around. If they were going to be married, her inheritance, her problems, would be Jax's as well.

The thought lifted her spirits some more. Romantic love, sex, they were aspects of life, but there were so many other facets as well. Like having someone who came running when they heard a tone in your voice.

Jax came back up front, his brows raised. "You'll want to have the vessel checked out by a professional, but from what I can see, the bones are actually in decent shape. And there's no dry rot. You could invest minimally to get it cleaned up, have the interior remodeled, and…"

"Save a life," Priscilla blurted, finding pieces of herself again as she smiled up at him. "I don't need a boat," she told him. "We have a stocked boathouse on the estate, but there's this program…you donate a car or a boat and they go up for bid and all the money goes to various programs for at risk children around the state. Linc's last act on earth could save lives!" She smiled and stood.

Just as Jax came forward. His gaze still holding hers, he stopped just inches from her and said, "You might just become addictive, Priscilla Fortune," then lowered his head and kissed her.

The brush of his lips against hers was brief. Asexual.

The touch of a friend.

Not a lover.

Priscilla was comforted, even as she was more aware than ever that she had some serious thinking to do.

And a major life choice to make.

One that would affect three lives, not just one.

Chapter Fifteen

Jax suggested dinner in town. Not to be seen. Or to gather witnesses. But because being out in public put off the sudden intimacy that had invaded the polite-but-providing-ample-distance mansion in which he'd grown up.

Over dinner, a sumptuous Italian feast through which Liam slept, he kept the conversation on Linc. Partially because he sensed that Priscilla needed to talk about the boy she'd known. To work through the segue to the man he'd become. And because he'd heard snippets of the mystery floating through their circle, the murder of the Fortunes' longtime housekeeper's son.

He also was a little curious to know if Priscilla had any lingering feelings for the man. She'd known him her whole life and then had gone out with him that summer. Rumor had it that she'd been hurt when he'd blown her off afterward. He'd heard that much before she'd intimated as much during one of their first conversations that week.

Christa had talked about a man who'd hurt her, too. The number the guy had done on her was what had driven her to playing the field. Choosing casual affairs over deeper connections. And yet, when she'd become pregnant, needing to settle down, Jax hadn't been enough for her…

And when, no matter how much Priscilla talked about

the man, he couldn't get a feel for whether her feelings were more that of losing a family member or a lover, he told himself to just let it go. It wasn't like he was going to keep her to her word to marry him.

With her fork in her right hand, she'd lifted her left one to reach for a roll, and he noticed the rock on her finger again. As he'd been doing since they'd been shown to their quiet, secluded booth.

"Were you in love with him?" The words came forth, and Jax was not pleased with himself. Even as he stopped eating while he waited for her response.

"Not at all," she said so easily, he felt tension slide out of him. "He'd shunned us all from the time we were teenagers. I was only in town for a few days, and I was more just glad to meet up with him long enough to see that he was doing okay."

Her face clouded and he asked, "But you wanted to go out with him again?"

She shrugged. "I wanted to keep in touch. To be friends."

To be friends. Because that was Priscilla. There if you needed her. Or wanted her to be. Which boded well for a future for him with her permanently in it.

And put far more responsibility on him to make certain that he didn't abuse her kindness to the point of robbing her of what *she* needed.

A fact of which he reminded himself later as, with Liam bathed and in his crib, Priscilla suggested a glass of wine before bed. Following her downstairs he found himself staring at her pert backside, thinking he could easily look at that for the rest of his life, and knew that he was in danger of making a mistake he would later regret.

She'd brought some wine in with her bearing the Fortune's Vintages label—her older brother's small but prestigious winery—and Jax retrieved the crystal wineglasses as she uncorked the bottle.

And when she raised her glass to his, he toasted with her as she said, "To living every day to its fullest."

He sipped, watching her over the rim of his glass. Intrigued, wanting to know, after the day she'd had, what she'd consider a full day. But said, "I'm not going to hold you to our engagement."

He hadn't planned the exact words, or when he'd say them. Probably hadn't chosen the best time. But he stood by the proclamation. And when she did nothing but take another sip of wine, and stare in front of her, he added, "You want more from me than I am, Priscilla. I'm not the guy who falls in love. Who even knows how to *be* in love. I just don't roll that way. And while you said you weren't looking for love either, this week has changed that for you, hasn't it?"

He wasn't kidding himself that she had fallen for him. The idea of it was too much for him to take on. But from what she'd said, he had a feeling it could happen at some point.

She'd turned her head. Was looking at him. Still silent.

"You want more," he pressed.

And with a sip of wine and lift of her chin, she admitted, "I've had some eye-opening moments, yes." And that was it. None of her usual wordiness. Filled with explanations he didn't always grasp.

Which meant no chance at all that he could grab hold of his next best move. So he waited.

"Being here in Emerald Ridge, falling in love with

Liam, watching the Noveltys grieve together while moving forward, Linc's shocking choice…and spending time with you…has shown me parts of myself I'd lost. And made me more aware of how precious life is."

He swallowed. Was sure that he was missing something huge. "And more susceptible to being hurt," he gritted out.

He'd be a selfish bastard to marry her.

Lifting a hand palm up, she seemed to concede his point. Then said, "Pain's a part of life, Jax."

"Which is why you do all you can to avoid as much of it as possible." Finally, something upon which he was completely clear. And there was more. "Another reason why I have to be certain that I minimize every possibility of my causing pain to others."

She looked at him, held his gaze, and he didn't even blink. He couldn't. She had to understand. To walk away.

And when she did? And the Noveltys came after Liam? He couldn't let himself jump that far ahead. Not at the risk of making Priscilla's life less than it was meant to be.

As his father had done to his mother. Rufus's talk had been with him all day. Showing him more things he hadn't seen before. His father had loved his mother. Enough to stay married to her for life. To provide for her. Be kind to her. Raise a family with her. Spend holidays and a lot of dinnertimes with her. But not enough to be faithful to her.

Something he'd hated himself for in the end.

Jax still had the chance to prevent himself from making the biggest mistake of his life.

Priscilla held his gaze. Until she didn't. Taking a sip of her wine, her gaze seemed to focus on the glass as she set it down. Then lifted her eyes back up to him. "Are you kicking me out?"

"Hell no!" The response bolted out. "This house was a morgue without you today," he added inanely, wanting only to assure her that he wasn't rejecting her. Quite the opposite. He was telling her she was worth more than what he had to provide.

Giving her the honesty that he'd vowed to give. Which was the purpose for the conversation to begin with.

But he knew he'd made a mistake, too, when he saw the gleam enter her eyes.

He watched as Priscilla nodded, jutted her chin, tossed a strand of that luscious long blond hair over her shoulder and pinned him with those hazel eyes. "Just so that I'm clear, the offer of marriage, the engagement is still on."

Well, no, it *shouldn't* be.

Before he could find a proper response, she continued with, "Because unless you're breaking off our engagement, which you have every right to do, it almost sounds as though you're trying to make my decisions for me, and that wasn't part of the deal. Honesty and truth. That's what we agreed upon."

He nodded. No argument there.

"So…you've been honest. You aren't reneging on your offer of marriage, which would then put Liam's custody immediately at risk, I might add. And if I choose to not rescind my acceptance of your proposal, that's *my* choice to make."

Of course, but he sat there, his gaze locked with hers, and…had no response. Except, "I don't feel good about taking my own happiness, and that of my son's, at the cost of yours."

She nodded. "And you think you're somehow in control of the choices I feel I need to make if you deem them counterproductive to my happiness?"

Jax shook his head. Sipped wine.

He'd met his match.

He just wished to hell he knew what he was supposed to do about it.

She was fighting for her life. Priscilla just wasn't sure what that life was supposed to be. The idea that Jax had been going to end their engagement had generated instant pushback.

No doubt in any part of her mind or heart that she did not want him to do that.

It was the one thing she was absolutely certain about. And so it was what she took upstairs with her when Liam cried out an hour after he'd gone to sleep. Jax had had the baby all day, and had to be out on the fence line at six in the morning. She'd missed her little guy as though she'd been away weeks, not hours, and claimed all of the night feedings.

Jax's concession had come with a long look, followed by a nod.

He'd gone into his office when she'd come upstairs, and fifteen minutes after she'd entered the nursery, with Liam rocked back to sleep, she didn't go back down. Uneasy that Liam had only slept for an hour—an indication of possible discomfort—she left the door between her room and the nursery open, and, with the book she'd been reading the night before in hand, settled on the couch in her room.

Priscilla had been losing herself in story for as long as she could remember, but that night, the characters on the page didn't reach out to her. She'd started the same paragraph over half a dozen or so times when she heard Liam whimper. Jumping up, she went in to him, rubbing his belly softly as he slept. Watching him.

Her heart filling with love.

That time when he settled, she sat in the rocking chair in the nursery, and was still there, dozing, half an hour later when Liam whimpered again. Immediately awake, she went to him, once again calmed him and sat back down.

He'd been out and about with Jax all day. Was probably just overtired. But she didn't want to take any chances. Nor did she want the baby to wake up his father.

She'd heard Jax come up shortly after she'd settled in the rocking chair. Had stiffened, waiting to see if he'd come in to tell his son good-night, and been disappointed when he hadn't done so, as though it somehow reflected on some need he might have to not risk running into her.

After the day she'd had—the week—her emotions were on overload. She could be forgiven for being a little more sensitive than usual.

And she needed to know that she and Jax were okay. That he still trusted her to be the wife she'd promised him she'd be. One who didn't—and wouldn't—expect more from him than he had to give...

The thought broke off as she heard a slight creak—the door from Jax's room into the nursery opening. From the shadows in the corner, she watched him take one slow, quiet, barefooted step. Then another. His hair was wet. And when he made it all the way around the end of the crib, she saw that he was dressed only in a pair of loose-fitting gym shorts.

He hadn't opted not to come in to tell Liam good-night after all. He'd just taken a shower first.

And she didn't want him to go.

Not without knowing they were really okay.

She also didn't want him to know she was there. Because she had nothing new to add to their conversation.

So she sat, hardly breathing, watching the tall, broad-shouldered man, lean down tenderly, whisper something to his son, lightly touch his forehead, then quietly leave the room.

Taking a piece of her with him.

He'd seen her sitting there. Too late to back out of the room without being noticed. Not wanting to interrupt whatever she'd been finding in that chair, that room, he told Liam good-night, and left the two of them alone.

But the vision of her sitting there stayed with him. That night and through the next few days, too. He'd be galloping across a pasture, and see Priscilla in the shadows, sitting in a darkened corner watching his son sleep.

Or securing new fencing, and remember Priscilla in the nursery, not making a sound.

After their talk, such as it was, on Sunday night, they'd reverted to the relationship they'd shared early on the previous week. They talked—just not about them or any personal feelings they might or not be capable of having. They ate together.

And each night, he'd retreat to his office, while she went up to bed. He'd follow soon after, but stay in his room until his four in the morning feeding time. If it came. Liam had been sleeping more at night. Four to six hour stretches even.

The beginning of a new phase.

The ending of one, too.

Priscilla hadn't said any more about setting a wedding date. He hadn't asked. The choice was hers.

But every day he found himself looking at her left hand, and finding peace in the diamond still glistening there.

He was also engaging in a whole lot of cold showers. He'd never been turned on by a woman as hotly as Priscilla was able to arouse him, but then, he'd never lived with one before, either.

Sex was another thing they didn't discuss. Not even in general terms.

True to her word, she'd stocked their wine supply. Not that they were drinking much of it. He'd taken to having a beer in his office at night, to wind down before going upstairs. And was otherwise abstaining. Just in case the wine had driven him to forget everything but joining his body with Priscilla's that last time they were together.

Based on how often he was getting hard around her, he wasn't thinking so, but it helped to be doing something to effect positive change, just in case change was possible.

As the week came to a close, he was beginning to settle in to the new normal. To relax and accept the way his life was going to feel. To let the future take care of itself.

Friday evening, after Liam was in bed, he was surprised when Priscilla didn't go straight to her room. She came down to his office instead. Entering after a very brief knock. "You got a minute?"

Dread filled his gut, but he nodded. What else could he do? He owed her all the minutes of his time she was ever going to need.

The fact that she was wearing the same silk robe she'd had on the first night they'd made love did not help. Instantly aroused as he imagined those sheer shorts and spaghetti strap top that made up the rest of the ensemble under that robe, he reached for his bottle of beer. Downed a quarter of it.

If she'd come to tell him she was leaving, he wouldn't argue. As devastating as it would be to have her gone, it was probably for the best.

Sitting on the couch to the left of his desk, she sipped from the glass of wine she'd brought in with her, threw a long lock of her hair over her shoulder and said, "I'd like to set a date for the wedding."

Relief was heady, flooding his body, his brain, leaving him powerless to do anything but smile. Drunkenly, it felt like.

"My family's asking. Zara wants to help plan the wedding, and I'd like to move forward as well. We've established a working relationship. You need this marriage, Jax. And I know that it's the best choice for me as well. I want Liam to officially be my son."

Good. Great! He continued to sit there with a ridiculous smile on his face. Unable to express any doubts as to the marriage being the best thing for her because she'd made it clear that that particular choice, or concern, wasn't in his wheelhouse.

"So, do you have a preference of dates? We can put our calendars together and figure out what works best for both of us."

"I don't want a big wedding." The words fell out. The truth. But not anything worth making an issue over.

"Yeah, I don't, either, which is why I think it's best that

we do this soon. And quietly. My family might be disappointed, but ultimately, they just want me happy, and with Roth's wedding on the horizon, they'll still get their big celebration."

Soon. The big wedding wasn't going to be an issue.

"I'd actually just like to go to the courthouse, meet with a judge and get it done," she said then. Describing, in his mind, the perfect wedding.

Christa had insisted on all the trappings. As had her parents. She was their only child, and Emma had been dreaming of the big, splashy wedding probably as long as Christa had. In retrospect, Jax was glad he'd given it to them.

"I can't believe you don't want a fancy wedding," he said quietly, then. If Priscilla had one fault, it was that she sacrificed herself far too much. "This relationship isn't going to work if you don't speak up for yourself," he said, warming up some. "Honesty, remember?"

Taking a sip of wine, she held his gaze, and then confided softly, "My father's not here to give me away. There is no mother of the bride. And while Uncle Sander and the rest of them would give a thousand percent to make the day perfect, I feel like I'd be settling for second best, and I don't want to start our life together that way." She swallowed. Licked her lips. Then said, "What I would like, after your sister returns, is a big reception, here, in our home. With a band and delicious food, champagne, lots of laughter and us celebrating the once in a lifetime friendship we've found together."

The words hit him in the gut. So hard he couldn't draw breath at first. He opened his mouth to tell her that it couldn't happen. But the picture she'd painted sounded so good, the words wouldn't spew forth.

"I've never had a friend as close as you've become in just these couple of short weeks," he said instead. Honesty. Trust.

He'd never spilled his guts to anyone as much as he had with her.

She smiled, as though she'd read his thoughts. At the moment, he wasn't sure she couldn't. It was like the woman knew exactly what he needed and so gave it to him.

While he sat around and took from her. With no ability to give back. To fulfill her needs. And he just couldn't do it.

"What do you get from the relationship?" he pretty much demanded. Because he had to show her that she was ruining her life.

If he wasn't man enough to send her away, he had to at least help her save herself. Even that seemed like nonsense to him. He had to break it off with her. Should never have accepted her offer in the first place.

"I don't know yet," she answered.

He stood, came around the desk, sat on the edge of the armchair across from her and said, "Then we *can't* do this, Priscilla. Not even for Liam. What if you meet someone who can give you the things you most want? Someone who's capable of loving you to distraction—"

He broke off at the word. She'd never once expressed a need, or desire, to be loved to distraction. He wasn't going to help her see his point unless he stayed on track.

"I've met my someone," she said then.

Jax's heart seemed to skip a beat. His gut filled with

rock. Mouth open, he fell back in the chair and took long slow breaths.

"Who?" What did it matter? He didn't want to know.

"Liam," she told him. And while he was grappling with that one, she added, "And you."

No. He stood. Backed away. She couldn't love him. They'd only been together two weeks. And…she just *couldn't* feel that way about him.

"You're the best friend I've ever had, Jax. I trust you in a way I've never trusted anyone. I say what I think, and you want that. You're honest with me.

"And you share your son with me. Wholeheartedly, no reservations. That's what I need. That's what you give me."

She hadn't said the word *love* while listing her needs. But he saw it, shining from her eyes. He stood there, staring at her, at the emotion written all over her and had to say, "What if I don't love you?"

A grin, of all things, lurked on the edges of her mouth as she said, "You in love with some other woman?"

"Of course not." He wasn't playing games.

She shrugged. "Then what's the issue?"

He'd just told her he didn't love her. That was the issue. "But you hope that, given time, I will."

He had her. Finally. He saw her eyes harden. Watched her stand and approach him, stopping only when her nose was inches from his. "You putting words in my mouth again, Jax? Thinking for me? Because it's insulting."

Fire burned from her eyes. Something he hadn't seen before.

Something he liked.

Because it set him free.

Fire meant fight. And it was blazing from the eyes pointed up at him.

It wasn't that she was subverting herself in order to please. She was fighting for what she wanted.

Him. Just as he was.

And God help him, he wanted her.

More than any woman he'd ever known.

Right then.

Right there.

Chapter Sixteen

Mad enough to act out, even though it was beneath her, Priscilla reached forward and planted her hand along Jax's fly. Pressing, she felt the hardness she'd known would be there. Wrapped her fingers around it as much as his jeans allowed. And said, "You going to deny that you want me, too?"

She almost shrieked when he bent and lifted her up into his arms. "Nope, I might be dense, but I'm an intelligent man," he said, then strode with her up the stairs.

He didn't take her to her room. He took her to his, undressed as quickly as he could, and, laying her back on his bed, leaned over her, unable to contain his urgent wanting.

She'd unleashed him. Which fed Priscilla's hunger in a way she'd never have expected. He wasn't rough with her. Nor was she with him. They were just mutually hungry.

Everything about them was urgent. Their kisses, the way their tongues met and clashed. Instead of feeling her up, his thumbs went straight to her nipples, tantalizing her. And, rising up over him, giving him freer access, she pressed her knee into his crotch.

Gently. And firmly, too.

Moving her leg up and down. Driving him to mindless passion with her.

Less than five minutes after they'd entered the room, he was sheathed from his own stash and inside her. And before they knew it, they convulsed together.

It wasn't until it was over, and they were lying there in the dark, recovering, that she realized, they still hadn't set a wedding date.

Giving Jax a few more minutes to regroup, she was surprised to hear his even breathing, even the tiniest bit of a snore.

The man had fallen asleep.

Frustrated, and also a little pleased with herself, she continued to lay there, learning what her soon to be husband sounded like when he slept.

And thought back over the past hour. The conversation she'd purposely forced. After a week of proving that they could make their relationship work—and growing more certain with each day that passed that she was right where she wanted to be—she'd been hell-bent on getting on with it.

They'd gotten on all right.

Just not exactly in the way she'd envisioned.

She'd almost jumped up and left when Jax had pushed the whole love issue. Because he'd clearly figured out, even before she'd said anything, that she was in love with him.

Not something she could change. Or help.

Love just...*was*.

But he was wrong to think that she'd be happier without him than she would be living without him loving her back. And yeah, she could possibly spend the rest of her days hoping he'd return her feelings. But it wasn't like leaving him would change that.

She'd done a lot of soul-searching over the past week. Taking Liam to her cottage, walking around both estates with him in his stroller. Singing to him.

She could leave Jax and the baby behind. Go back to life as it had been before she'd known them. Living alone, engaging in meaningless dating, in the hope of someday meeting someone who would replace Jax in her life.

But she knew it wasn't going to happen. She might find another man to care about. Might even agree to marry him. But in her heart, she'd be comparing him to Jax Wellington, and that wouldn't be right.

Or...she could marry Jax. Take the bad with the good. Live with him and Liam, with her heart filled with love. Her love for both of them. And bask in the caring, the honesty, the wanting that Jax gave back to her. She might not be the love of his life, but she'd forever be his best friend.

There'd be other bridges to cross.

Her desire to have a baby with him someday. But whether he agreed to another child or not didn't change the rest.

She wasn't going to be like Linc. Throwing away the advantages he'd had, spurning the people who'd have shared their wealth with him, giving him whatever steps up he'd needed to feel rich enough, just because he'd decided he had to get there himself. To prove...she had no idea what.

His need to attain whatever fantasy image he'd somehow formed in his head growing up had driven the man to criminal activity.

And it would be equally criminal for Priscilla to walk away from the love in her heart.

She crept back to her own room, though. She was cold and needed to crawl under the covers. Or so she told herself.

Mostly, she hadn't wanted to lie on the top of Jax's covers feeling abandoned, without being held, or kissed good-night, after sex.

She'd get used to his ways in time. She was certain of that.

In the meantime, she just needed a few minutes alone to let the tears drip slowly down her cheeks.

And then she'd be fine.

Jax woke up as Priscilla slid off his bed. He wasn't sure why he'd let her go. Something perverse within him that wouldn't let him attempt to be more than he'd been built to be.

He heard her blow her nose, shortly thereafter, too. Softly. Almost undetectably. Had he not been lying there all senses tuned to the woman in her room, he wouldn't have noticed. Or been aware of the second and third time.

Unless she'd suddenly developed a head cold, or some allergy that didn't include sneezing, Priscilla was crying.

Because of him.

A couple of hours ago, he'd have marched in that room, broken their engagement and been done with the whole damned mess he made of her life, freeing her to build something so much better.

But life just wasn't that easy.

While he didn't understand a lot of what Priscilla had been trying to help him to grasp over the past couple of weeks, he'd gotten enough that evening to know that she needed him.

That his friendship was as invaluable to her as hers was to him.

That it would be cruel to take Liam from her.

And yet…as painful as ripping all of that away from her would be…she'd get over them. Move on. There'd be scars, but she'd heal.

And someday meet someone who would cherish her enough to make her forget she ever knew them.

Or…he could marry her.

And sentence her to a life of crying alone in her bed at night.

As though heaven was knocking him on the head, Liam let out a wail right then, and Jax was up, pulling on shorts as he rushed into the nursery, grabbing the baby up quickly enough to alert Priscilla that he was on duty.

Even though it was her turn.

She showed up anyway. Her robe tightly tied around her. No sign of a tissue—or tears—in sight.

She was hiding from him. And through the years, it would only get worse.

Turning his back on her, he faced the changing table and got Liam wiped, dry and re-dressed. Then slowly spun back, expecting to see her gone.

Instead, she stood there, holding a warmed bottle. Just as he'd done for her in the past.

He took the bottle. Sat in the rocking chair. Fed the nipple between his son's tiny lips before Liam got pissed and let him know about it. Gearing up for a talk he didn't want to have.

"We didn't set a wedding date." Priscilla's words fell like deadweight in the room. As though, once again, she'd read his mind.

Or knew him well enough to figure out his intent.

Quietly, watching Liam, he said, "I don't think we should."

Then waited for the smart words to come shooting back at him. Letting him know that he couldn't make her choices for her.

Almost hoping that she'd have some magic bullet stashed away that would buy him a little more time.

But knowing deep down that he would only be prolonging the inevitable if he gave into it.

Yet still he waited.

Until he felt tension building to the point of compelling an answer from her and glanced up to somehow tell her it was over.

Only to see an empty doorway.

She was gone.

Softly closing the door to her room, Priscilla climbed into bed and went to sleep. She woke for Liam's 3:00 a.m. feeding, left the six o'clock one to Jax, listening to make sure he was awake and tending to Liam, then started to pack her trunk.

Just as she had the right to make her own decisions, the right to control her own life, so did he. No matter what she thought of his reasoning.

The man did not feel good about marrying her.

And so they shouldn't wed.

His soft knock on her door twenty minutes later shocked her. Freezing, a pile of underwear in her hand suspended over one end of the trunk, she stared at the knob. Then remembered Liam, her responsibility to the baby until Jax had a chance to make other arrangements, and said quietly, "Come in."

She gave him one glance. Then closed her half-packed

trunk, not wanting her personal items exposed, before turning back to him.

He was looking down at it, his face mostly expression-less. "You were crying."

She wasn't sure she'd heard him right at first. Then re-alized that as quiet as she'd thought she'd been, he'd obvi-ously been aware of her tears the night before.

"I do that now and then," she told him. "Ever since I was a baby. Though not nearly as often now that I'm an adult." Her tone bordered on sarcasm, but didn't quite get there.

"I don't." He looked her right in the eye as he spoke, as though those two words ended the conversation. And them.

If he thought she was going to beg, he was going to be disappointed.

They were either both in, or there was no point in going forward. Up until she'd gone into the nursery the night before, she'd just thought he was being the man she'd come to know—one who took care of his responsibilities, who always stood up and did the right thing, even when it meant marrying a woman he'd been about to break up with because she was carrying his baby.

She'd thought—because he'd told her so—that his aver-sion to their union was based on his belief that she wasn't getting what she needed out of it. That he'd been spar-ing her.

But his words in the nursery…saying that he didn't think they should set a wedding date…they'd been dif-ferent. Emphatic.

Like he'd made up his mind.

Still looking at her trunk, Jax approached the bed, and

Priscilla stepped away. Around the end of the bed, to stand there and watch as he pushed aside her case and sat down.

"I don't know what to do, Priscilla," he confessed. "We made lifelong decisions overnight. I made everything public in our relatively small circle. I got the Noveltys involved. I'm responsible for getting Christa pregnant, which means Liam is *my* responsibility. And you're like this breath of fresh air that I wish to God I'd met before all of this…"

She half chuckled, with no humor at all. "You had met me, but we had nothing in common. I don't like to jet set. It's all you did back then. Life happens to us, Jax. It changes people. Liam changed you. And me, too." She huffed out a breath. "If you're lucky, you have a few people in your world who go with the changes, who stick by you through the years. And if you're more than lucky? You meet someone who travels the whole journey with you, changing with you, as the years dole out their bounty and hardships. It's a crapshoot."

She was babbling. Mostly speaking out loud the things the past couple of weeks had taught her. Things that, before Jax and Liam, she hadn't been ready to face.

"I made you cry."

"Yep. And I can pretty much guarantee it won't be the last time." Most particularly if he ended what they'd begun.

Taking a seat on the small couch, she leaned forward, her arms crossed over her chest, and said, "You're looking at all the bad, Jax. The negatives. Why not look at the good this relationship is bringing me? I'm happier now, *truly happy*, not just staying busy happy. My life finally has deeper purpose. My heart is filled, with Liam, and yes, with you, too. Love's funny like that. It doesn't require payback. And...as an added bonus...the sex is phenomenal."

His lips quirked and she just kept talking. "The practicality of our situation, the way we came at it, while certainly different than the norm, actually works for me. I *like* that emotions are not the sole source of our commitment. Honesty and trust give me the security that I need."

He glanced at her trunk. "Then why are you packing?"

"Because you aren't all in. It's not just about love, Jax, it's about commitment. You're not comfortable with us, our situation, our commitments. And that I can't live with." She hadn't been planning to go very far, at first. Just to the next wing of his home while they figured out the future. And if they were splitting, how to handle the Noveltys.

Liam's future mattered more to her than her own. She couldn't choose his suffering as justified sacrifice for her own ultimate comfort and well-being.

And...oh...her heart dropped as understanding dawned. With the force of a ton of bricks.

Jax couldn't take his and Liam's happiness over her well-being, either. He couldn't live with himself, any more than she could embrace reaching for her own needs at the cost of directly making someone else suffer.

And that was their breaking point.

Chapter Seventeen

Jax carried Priscilla's trunk to the other wing in the stately mansion that had been his home most of his life. It had been thoroughly cleaned, painted and refurbished since Courtney's arrest. He'd had it done the first week he'd moved in. Most of the furnishings had been stored when Courtney had insisted on buying all new things.

He'd donated her "new" items to a housing project for those on fixed incomes that he'd helped finance in Houston after he'd first left Emerald Ridge.

The baby monitor didn't reach that far, so he'd be handling all of the nighttime feedings again, while Priscilla, with Sasha's help, continued to care for Liam during the day.

The housekeeper's meals would continue to feed them both.

And he didn't like any of it. Not one bit.

He'd had a door built for Priscilla, and she wasn't using it. The room she'd occupied felt morgue-like.

He was supposed to be feeling a whole lot better about himself, with her having taken the first step to separating from him—the man she loved who couldn't love her back.

Monday and Tuesday, he immersed himself in work on the ranch. In addition to all of the fencing that Courtney had sabotaged, she hadn't paid attention to the herd, and Wellington Beef had a reputation that Jax was not going to have tarnished.

The people who'd come from the ranch—his dad, him, Annelise—might not all be the best in the west, but their cattle were. To that end, he was having every head checked over, and had also started to expand their breeding operation. More heads, more excellence.

He missed Priscilla at dinner. Ended up eating in his office. And heading up to bed early as had become his routine since single-fatherhood had been thrust upon him. He'd seen her car leave both evenings. And though they texted during the day—her giving him regular photos and updates on Liam and him thanking her—he didn't ask where she went when she was off duty. And she didn't share.

They'd agreed to keep up appearances of an engagement still in the works, with a wedding planned for late fall. Before their marriage license would be null and void. They'd agreed to take the extra time so that their breakup wouldn't make them both look totally irresponsible in having gotten engaged at all.

Or, they hoped, tip-off the Noveltys to the whole thing being fake to begin with. An arrangement to get them to drop their custody battle.

Jax worried a lot about that over the next days. Not only had he not loved their daughter, Christa, but the Noveltys were sure to blame him for parting ways with Priscilla, too. He had to wonder if it would sway a judge in their direction, too, since the engagement was so quick to begin with.

He had a lot of time to think—too much of it—as he

rode fence line and herded cattle. And found himself seeking out the company of his ranch hands just to get away from whatever was pushing his brain into overload.

Yeah, in a lot of ways, it had been a great couple of weeks with Priscilla, but he'd had other fabulous times in his life as well and had never had trouble walking away from them.

But then, he'd never had anyone else but himself involved. This time around, he had a helpless, completely dependent young life depending on him to get it right.

The weight of that responsibility was what had prompted him to end things with Priscilla. To set her free. He didn't want his son looking back on his youth and seeing a father who didn't love his mother.

As Jax had done.

And he also didn't want to be putting his fist through a wall someday because he hated himself for hurting Priscilla all those years.

He was just coming around an acre of trees, ready to hit open pasture where some of his men were rounding up cattle when he heard, "...urgent call." Then, "big guy's fiancée" followed by something he couldn't make out and had his heels in his horse's sides, slapping the reins with rapid quick taps, and clicking his tongue against his teeth, racing back toward the house.

He had to get there. Had to get to her before they took her away. Had to be with her...

Jax had no thoughts, allowed no others, but to get to Priscilla as fast as humanly possible. To will her to hang on. To wait for him to be by her side.

And he prayed for her life. Over and over. Begging the

powers that be to let her feel him—if such a thing was possible. For her to know that he coming to her.

She had to know.

It would make a difference to her.

There was no introspection. No thoughts of past or future. Right or wrong. Just the now.

Which consisted of one thing.

Keeping Priscilla alive.

Priscilla was in the garden room, reading while Liam slept in his swing. Allowing herself to enjoy the moments without thoughts of the future. Sasha had been there that morning, and Priscilla had gone into town to have her hair conditioned, trimmed and shaped, but had been home by lunchtime.

She wasn't ready to answer any questions—to deal with gushing over her new engagement—or to think about her future. Not wanting to spend any more time in Courtney's wing than she had to, she'd gone to her mini mansion each evening. Hadn't sought out or seen anyone.

Nor would anyone know she'd been there alone.

Her family, if they'd even seen her car come and go, was allowing her and Jax their space as they formed their new life together. She loved them for that.

And was giving herself time to just be. With her past. Her present. All of the feelings that had come surging forth over the past few weeks. Instigated, she now knew, by her love for Liam and then Jax. Fueled by the deep emotional memories she'd allowed to resurface.

She was in control of what she could control. And coming to terms with the fact that she couldn't have authority over every single thing that happened to her. Or affected her deeply. She could just do her best to manage her response to them. To make choices that suited her life, and the world, in the best possible way.

Like the choice to text Jax when the Noveltys arrived over the past weekend. Maybe the choice had been the beginning of their demise. He'd certainly seemed more spooked afterward.

Which might have just been coincidental and had nothing at all to do with the older couple. The fact that seeing them interact with each other in such difficult circumstances had touched her deeply didn't mean that it had had the same effect on him.

Still, seeing him coming galloping toward the house... she turned her head, staring out the same window she'd been watching for him through that Saturday morning... had given her a start. A big one. Remembering how her heart had lurched, and settled then, how having him there with her had felt like coming home, she knew that she was home.

She loved him. Because he was the only one for her and she'd just had to meet him to know she had the capacity? Maybe. Probably.

That was how love worked. When the time was right.

Certainly her overhearing the initial conversation between him and Emma and Frank in the park that morning had been more than coincidence.

Feeling a jolt pass through her, she blinked. She'd thought she'd seen Jax galloping their way. Right then. Not just in Saturday's memory replay. Blinking a second time, she stared, hard, at the landscape that seemed to be placidly and peacefully living another day.

Minus any sign of horse and rider.

She'd just told herself to get out of her head and back to her book, reminding herself of the choice not to get lost in thought until more time had passed, giving her a chance for distance, and thus more clarity...when she heard, *"Priscilla! Sasha!"* and the sound of cowboy boots pounding on tile.

Blood draining from her face, she dropped her book and ran in the direction of the sound. "Jax?"

If he'd been hurt...or someone else had...she had to help him. "Jax?" she called again, running toward the kitchen where he'd likely go to find Sasha.

He'd called her name, though. She had to...

Rounding a corner, she crashed so fiercely into his form that she'd have fallen if he hadn't caught her. "Priscilla?"

His hands were on her shoulders, gripping a little too tightly, and he was staring at her as though he'd seen a ghost.

"Jax?" she called to him softly. Hoping to get him to focus. Clearly something horribly tragic had happened. She'd never seen him look so devastated. So...lost.

If she hadn't just seen Liam sleeping peacefully in his swing, she'd have been terrified herself. That boy was the only thing she could think of that would upset the staunch cowboy to that extent.

He blinked, his grip softening as his fingers started to rub her shoulders, over and over. Throat tight and mouth dry, she asked, "What's wrong? What happened?"

He shook his head. Rubbed both hands up and down the sides of her neck, holding her head still as he stared intently down at her. "You broke your neck," he told her inanely.

Fear gripped her, started to strip away her ability to think, as she grasped the idea that he'd been hurt. Had taken a fall. Hit his head.

"No, I didn't," she told him softly, needing Sasha there, someone to watch over Liam. "You need to lie down," she said then. She had no idea what he needed.

Had never been so scared.

"You didn't break your neck." Jax said the words as though he was reading them. "You're fine."

"Yeah, I'm fine. I've been sitting in the garden room reading. Liam's asleep in his swing."

"Reading," he echoed, his gaze seeming to come into focus. "Liam." He nodded then.

Let go of her. Stepped back. And just stood.

Looking more lost than anyone she'd ever seen.

Priscilla was fine.

Standing right there in front of him.

A very worried expression lining her beautiful face as she watched him. It hit him, then, how he must have looked, coming raging into the house ready to beat back the devil to get to his fiancée in time.

His fiancée.

Taking two steps forward, he grabbed her again, with both hands gently cupping the sides of her head, and bent his head, covering her lips with his own.

Sliding his tongue into her mouth and melting when hers joined in the dance he'd initiated.

He lifted his head for air then, and taking her hand, led her back to the garden room. He had to sit down.

And didn't want to let go of her.

Ever. Didn't ever again want to experience the terror that had filled him all the way across the pasture and past the barns. She went with him, half guiding him to the couch, and then sat down with him before he'd even indicated that he'd like her to do so. She was just there, naturally. Her thigh touching his.

"What's going on, Jax?" she asked, worry evident in her tone.

Which reminded him, some big guy's fiancée had a broken neck. And…like a lightning flash, he remembered something else he'd heard that morning while working with the same crew. Just a snippet. About some movie streaming in the bunkhouse the night before…a murder thriller.

Feeling like an absolute idiot, he pulled out his phone. Called Rufus. Asked the old guy if he'd been in the bunkhouse with the men the night before. And then asked about the movie that had been on.

And didn't wait around to hear the whole story. Just enough to know that he'd overreacted to the point of severe embarrassment. At the very least.

And, as he hung up, was thankful that no one but Priscilla had seen the evidence.

Right. Priscilla…

She was sitting there staring at him as though he'd lost his mind.

Which he very nearly had.

Getting it back wasn't all that much better.

It shoved him face-to-face with his own truths.

He was a damned coward. Afraid to love.

And…more afraid, infinitely afraid, of losing the woman he loved.

He stared, frozen, not sure what to do next.

Liam sighed loudly in his sleep. Though it was something the baby did regularly, Jax figured that time was no mistake, either. Apparently, it took an entire universe to get him to see the light.

"I heard some guys talking. I thought you'd fallen and were hurt."

She sat back, eyes wide, then slowly, her eyebrows rose.

"And you cared," she said, a smile teasing at the corners of her mouth.

Shaking his head, feeling a grin coming on, he rasped, "I guess it's pretty obvious that I did. Talk about a guy hitting himself over the head with his own lack of clarity..."

He stopped then, knowing that he couldn't let her play this one down. "I love you, Priscilla Fortune," he said, looking her straight in the eye, his tone dead serious. "I can't promise to make you happy, or be a good husband, but I can promise to spend every hour of every day trying."

"Right now. Because you were afraid I'd been hurt. But what about when I'm right here, every day, just fine and maybe getting in your way? What about when you're bored with the status quo? When the newness wears off?"

He figured he deserved the doubts. He'd been abundantly clear about his inability to stick with any one woman for long.

And gave her the truth. "Since I've never let anyone hang around long enough for that to happen, I can't say for sure. You know, in exact detail. But what I can tell you is that I want to find out. With you. I want you to be there. Showing me the way when I screw up. And hopefully showing you some things, too."

She stared up at him. Her eyes glistening. But still filled with doubt, too.

"You're different, Priscilla. The way I feel every single time I'm around you, thinking about you, or just peripherally aware that you're in my life… I've never felt anything like it."

"And when I make you angry? Then what?"

"Then I'm still right here. Working it out. I'm going to fight for you, for us, just as hard as I've been fighting for Liam. I didn't want to feel this way. But I do. It's there. And I'm not going to screw it up." He grew stronger with every word. Felt the truth of them. Or, if I do, I'll be here doing everything in my power to make it better. Until the day I die.

"I love you," he said again. Looking her right in the eye, letting his emotions shine for her to see.

And nearly crumpled when he heard her say, "I love you, too." With a hand to the side of his face, Priscilla added, "I'm not going to make you happy every minute of every day, either, Jax. It's called a *relationship*. It has ups and downs. But hopefully, the love is there to make everything better. That's where the saying comes from, you know, kiss it and make it better. And kiss and make up. And…"

Jax heard her loud and clear. Stopped her words with his lips to hers. Kissing her soundly. Knowing he was promising to spend the rest of his life by her side, facing whatever would come.

Together.

And didn't feel even a hint of fear. Or a need to vacate. Just like he'd known, when he'd heard that he was going to have a child, that he would be there for the child for the rest of his days.

Sliding down off the couch, onto one knee, he pulled his mouth from hers and said, "Priscilla Fortune, will you marry me? For real? Forever? As soon as possible?"

With tears in her eyes, she nodded, then said, "Yes. Tomorrow would work well for me. And see, you're making me cry again and the world isn't ending."

To the contrary it was just beginning.

And he was all in.

* * * * *

*Look for the next installment of the new continuity
The Fortunes of Texas: Fortune's Hidden Treasures*

Fortune for a Week

by USA TODAY *bestselling author
Nancy Robards Thompson
On sale October 2025,
wherever Harlequin books and ebooks are sold.*

And catch up with the previous books

His Family Fortune

*by New York Times bestselling author
Elizabeth Bevarly*

Available now!